FUM D'ESTAMPA PRESS

THE OTHERS

RAÜL GARRIGASAIT

TRANSLATED BY TIAGO MILLER

RAÜL GARRIGASAIT (Solsona, 1979) studied music and ancient languages, and writes essays and fiction. In 2017 he published his novel *Els estranys* (*The Others*), the winner of numerous literary prizes. Amongst other books, he has published the essays *El gos cosmopolita i dos espècimens més*, *Els fundadors*, *La ira* and *País barroc*. With one foot in the field of abstract reflection and the other in the telling of stories, Garrigasait forms part of a long tradition of meditation on the idols and issues of the modern world.

TIAGO MILLER (London, 1987) is a writer and translator living and working in Lleida, Catalonia. In addition to his translations of Catalan literature, he contributes articles on Catalan culture and language to various publications.

'*The Others* forces us to leave our comfort zone, and to steer away from indifference, banality, and conformity. A magnificent book!'
—Sam Abrams, *El Mundo*

'This fantastic book provides us with a reflection of our modern-day selves. The echoes with the present are so intense that it leaves you breathless after every phrase. *The Others* has the courage to force us to ask ourselves: "What skeletons lurk inside our cupboards?"'
—Toni Sala, *Ara*

'This majestic novel contains moments of tenderness, humour and violence. Garrigasait's writing is both precise and utterly brilliant, allowing us to take a closer look at a country and mentality that is still with us almost two centuries later.'
—Jordi Puntí, *El Periódico*

'With *The Others*, Garrigasait submerges us in a lucid clarity that is nothing less than marvellous.'
—Esteve Plantada, *Nació Digital*

FUM D'ESTAMPA PRESS LTD.
LONDON – BARCELONA
WWW.FUMDESTAMPA.COM

This translation has been published in Great Britain
by Fum d'Estampa Press Limited 2021

001

Els Estranys
by Raúl Garrigasait
Copyright © Edicions de 1984, 2015
All rights reserved
Translation copyright © Tiago Miller, 2021

The moral right of the author and translator has been asserted
Set in Minion Pro

Printed and bound by TJ Books Ltd, Padstow, Cornwall
A CIP catalogue record for this book is available from the British Library

ISBN: 978-1-913744-00-7

Series design by 'el mestre' Rai Benach

This work was translated with the help of a grant from the Institut Ramon Llull.

**LLLL institut
ramon llull**
Catalan Language and Culture

FUM D'ESTAMPA PRESS

THE OTHERS

To Helena, Mir and Joana.
To my friends.

I

A Slavic sounding surname, a sterile study room in a Berlin library, a childhood spent at 41 degrees, 59 minutes and 52 seconds north, 1 degree, 31 minutes and 15 seconds east: these are the three chance events that have led me to write these pages.

I first heard the name uttered one December evening, on such an occasion that it seemed to have been carefully prepared. I was having supper at the ancestral home of a legendary lineage of Carlist guerrillas called the Tristanys. We had gained entrance because the building – in reality, a fortress-like collection of three adjoining buildings in different architectural styles – had since been converted into a rural tourism destination. On the long table in the main hall was a spread consisting of cheeses, cured meats, sausages, ham, enormous slices of bread, ripe tomatoes, bottles of wine and spirits, all with an abundance that suggested a long, noisy night was in store. We talked non-stop, with the tiresome tendency to obsessively go over the same subjects, to continually cover the same ground, to emit loud cries which were nothing more than repetitions of things already claimed and cast aside. Given there were more than ten of us, three or four conversations had simultaneously sprung up around the table; when we got tired, we would move our chairs this way or that, or get up and go and stand by the fireplace (which the owners had not allowed us to light) to see if, amid a different conversation, we could clear our heads. Having found myself trapped beneath a deluge of denouncements of the powers that be, I sneaked away and stood at the top of the table, next to a stout man with a shaved head who emanated tranquillity; he was talking in hushed tones to his neighbour about the Carlists, like someone sharing a secret, and I had to lean in and concentrate in order to catch even a single word. The one I ended up catching sounded like some kind of friction interrupted by an explosion.

I was compelled to repeat it. It was a name: Lichnowsky.

The man told me that the memoirs of this gentleman, Prince Felix von Lichnowsky, Prussian, Catholic and quite possibly initiated into Freemasonry, amusingly evoked a world which was, to me at least, utterly incomprehensible: that of the First Carlist War. The fricative and plosive name struck a chord in me. I didn't know the first thing about him, yet I had the feeling he wasn't altogether unknown to me. A few days later, after I had recovered from the evening at the Tristany house, I realised I had read the name sometime before in Joan Perucho's best-known novel, *Natural History*. Lichnowsky appears in it as a devotee of belles-lettres and piccolo playing who, at twenty-three years of age, feels in his heart the full fervour of the royalist cause. Prone to insomnia and chivalry, while bivouacking on the banks of the Francolí he would lose himself in the contemplation of a locket bearing the ringlet of a married Italian woman. He had the misfortune of always turning up late to battles, when the Carlists had already been defeated, driven out, and pushed back towards the border. Storms terrified him.

Afterwards I learnt that, following the publication of his memoirs, Lichnowsky was challenged to a duel by a Spanish general, surviving only by the skin of his teeth, and that later, in 1848, when the March Revolution erupted in Germany, he was elected a member of the national parliament in Frankfurt. Taking his seat on the right among the representatives of the nation, he specialised in exquisitely scorning those who had most faith in progress, informing them with a pyrotechnic display of rhetoric that not only were they profoundly mistaken but that they were, in addition, deserving of boundless, physiological contempt. The more hate that came Lichnowsky's way, the greater his delight in ridiculing his enemies, until one day, as if overcome by a premonition, he delivered a relaxed, reasoned speech, a great rallying call in favour of reconciliation. That very same day there was another popular revolt. As he was leaving Frankfurt, a mob recognised him, gave chase, lost sight of him, found him again hiding in a gardener's shed and threw themselves upon him with guns and fists and teeth – like cannibals, some went as far as saying. Lichnowsky, in the prime of life, lay for a few hours in his death throes, his conscience clear, relishing it until the last.

Shortly after, a somewhat imprudent publisher got involved. We've all heard of publishers who are rolling in money, have friends in high places and suck like vampires on the creative blood of authors. The one I'm referring to wasn't of that particular breed. He was the type who earn their money with a regular day job and lose it publishing the books they are passionate about. These are sensitive creatures, capable of harbouring heartfelt grudges against the world, but as innocent as a child when stood before the beautiful curiosities accumulated by humanity.

About four months after that supper, I received an e-mail from said publisher with an offer to translate Lichnowsky's memoirs. Even coming from him the idea surprised me. In fact, it worried me. In his native Germany, Lichnowsky the author is impossible to find; who would be the slightest bit interested in reading him in these southern latitudes? But the work was reasonably well paid (not at all uncommon for projects involving publishers on the verge of bankruptcy) and I had time and a certain curiosity to know just what the book that had been hovering over me for months had to say. I accepted. I had a year to do it.

I dare say wasting your time when you have work to be getting on with is a universal pleasure. In any case, it's a pleasure that translators relish with delight. Perhaps it's because our work involves incomprehension, therefore delaying the job at hand is a way of showing solidarity with all the incongruities that both obstruct and stimulate communication. I have always tended to postpone the start of paid translations, to divert my attention, to dig deep into terrains related but not, strictly speaking, essential to the task. That same summer I had planned to spend a week in Berlin. It had been my own choice to go there but I couldn't say I was looking forward to it very much. Germany, yes – little would I have done in life if not for Germany –, but the capital had always seemed like a wasteland to me, a wide expanse of woodland and scrub with slices of city scattered over it. From one winter visit, I recall how the wind along the wide, deserted avenues wounded like a paralysing dart. I went there out of a certain sense of duty, or out of shame: everyone said that Berlin was one of the most interesting (they actually used words like 'in' and 'cool') cities in Europe, and I, who translated German for a living had, at a push, seen only a handful of its streets. I wasn't expecting to find anyone there: my three acquaintances in the city had all left, separately, for holidays along the Mediterranean coast.

One morning I was walking along the six lanes of traffic that make up the Potsdamer Straße. My natural instinct made me seek out small, narrow streets with calming limits, albeit to no avail. I had Lichnowsky's memoirs in my rucksack and the vague notion of stopping in some quiet corner to work for a few hours, even though all I really felt like doing was contemplating the world. I turned right between a row of trees and dozens of parked bicycles and found myself in front of the Staatsbibliothek. While standing in the doorway, caught between lethargy and indecision, a redhead with freckles flicked me one of those courteous smiles that girls from the north so readily offer and which fill introverts from the south with longing. I followed her inside. I'm not quite sure how, but she passed through security in a flash, whereas I had to deposit my mobile, belt and bag in a plastic tray under the watchful eye of a guard with a head the size of a watermelon. Once inside, I noticed the red-headed German girl had already vanished and that a woman was interrogating me with her gaze from behind a desk. I attempted to head towards some tables, but the position of the woman's eyebrow clearly indicated that I had made a wrong move.

'*Kann ich Ihnen helfen?*' Rather than offering help, she seemed to be reprimanding me.

Dozens of syllables rose up from my lungs but they all became lodged in my throat. Finally, the lid came off and out flowed the name that had been following me around for months, that long friction with an explosive end.

'Felix Fürst von Lichnowsky?'

Ten minutes later, at a table all to myself, I had in front of me a box file full of his family documents. As per usual, my initial feeling of wonder immediately gave way to apathy. Faced with so many papers, I had no idea where to begin or if I would even find anything of interest. But, peering out of the corner of my eye, at the very end of the file, I saw, to my surprise, a folder labelled CARLISTENKRIEG. For the benefit of enthusiasts of historical novels, I will add that, indeed, the pages were yellowed and dusty, but I assure you there were no burnt edges and none was written in any exotic or secret language. Despite the label, it turned out that these were not, in fact, notes written by Lichnowsky about his time in the army of Charles de Borbó; these belonged to someone else, to one Rudolf von Wielemann, according to the rubric. This man had written, in hasty German, notes concerning a whole manner of personal experiences from the years 1837 to 1838. My heart skipped a beat when I saw, on the first page, place names that were familiar to me.

The presence of those pages in that particular file must have been a mistake. I looked up at the woman behind the desk and kept quiet. I then began taking notes on his life. I'm still working on it. Over time it has exercised too much control over me, buried itself too deep inside, to not be shared in some shape or form.

Naturally, there are many details of Rudolf von Wielemann's biography that are impossible for me to know: entire tracts of his past appear to be permanently lost. His manuscript is a collection of diverse, often disconnected and at times indecipherable commentaries. In order to narrate this period of his life as he intended, I will have to behave as historians, economists, and scientists do: I will have to invent the connections myself. What other option do I have? It's my only way of explaining what I know for sure. Objects and events are mute; it's our words that make them speak, our truthful fictions.

No one cares about this obscure Prussian, you say? Alright, no one cares. All the more reason to talk about him.

The centre of all those place names jotted down by a stranger the best part of two centuries ago was at 41 degrees, 59 minutes and 52 seconds north, 1 degree, 31 minutes and 15 seconds east. From an extraterrestrial's perspective, there's nothing remarkable about this geographical point: it's not the centre of some large expanse of land such as Greenland. Nor does it occupy a pre-eminent position like Cape Town or Petropavlovsk-Kamchatsky. The most logical way to find it is to first fix your gaze on the vast Asian landmass and then turn it towards the tiny appendage we call Europe. Between the continuation of the Asian continent and the African coast, at the western limit of the oily lagoon that forms there, this cosmic being would discover the accumulation of asphalt and cement and suspended particulate matter heralded by the name of Barcelona. At this point the path becomes wayward. More accustomed to accidents of nature than human constructions, the extraterrestrial would do well to follow a more primordial, aquatic route. With the sea to its back and turning left, leaving behind miles and miles of concrete and tarmac, it would arrive in the wetlands of the Llobregat where, continuing to advance upriver between cars and the subdued hills, it would then skirt an enormous bare wart made of sedimentary rock with two monasteries perched on top of it. Here, humans will already have started to become thin on the ground and the woods to spread out like an endless carpet. After tracing three S-shaped curves it would then come to a watery junction where it would take the River Cardener on its left, flowing closely past clusters of houses, a tortuous highway, salt mountains, castles both ruined and restored, and forsaken farmhouses. At another tiny turnoff it would similarly take a left but what it would find there, despite being called the River Black, would appear more like a stream. There would be little, if any, water and the visitor's long, pointed toes would sink into the soft, cool mud. Wading in zigzags, it would pass an imposing and ancient tower resisting the weight of the centuries as best it could and, advancing obstinately along a riverbed getting narrower and muddier with each step, it would finally fix its eyes, nose, fingers, or some other unclassifiable member upon the two large tanks of the municipal sewage works. Now all that remains would be to continue for a few hundred metres in a straight line between the reeds, weeds, and rheumatic willows, with an effort born out of faith, a faith worthy of even the most self-sacrificing of anthropologists. Catching sight of a three-arched bridge, the extraterrestrial would stand up covered in mud and faecal sludge and now be at 41 degrees, 59 minutes and 52 seconds north, 1 degree, 31 minutes and 15 seconds east, looking at a blue dome, a high, encrusted wall and a gateway with a golden plaque representing the sun. This would be the entrance to a proud city, cut off from the world, accustomed to concealing with a ceremonious air the darkest moments in its history: the remote diocese of Solsona.

2

Two long columns of infantry marched ahead, panting heavily in an effort to curb their sweating. Counts, marquises, generals and the Infante Sebastian followed on horseback. Behind them on a white horse, wearing a broad sun hat, a black parade tunic, and olive-coloured riding breeches, advanced Don Charles Maria Isidre de Borbó. Under a blistering morning sun, the monarch divined grey stone and bell towers in the distance; he tried to sharpen his vision, but the city appeared like a shapeless rock covered in stalagmites stretching absurdly towards the sky. The king resisted the urge to quicken the pace in order to sooner escape the sweltering summer heat. "Sovereign composure befitting a monarch", he repeated to himself, under the watchful eye of the heavens above and his royal escort below. He heard the soldiers curse in Castilian, Catalan and Basque yet, despite sharing their complaints, their profanities upset him.

Hordes of black dots, as restless as feasting flies, were cramming into the Llobera Gate. The soldiers shouted at them to make way while announcing the king's arrival with cries of "*Viva el rey!*" Don Charles sat upright on his horse, puffed out his chest and proceeded to smooth down his moustache. He relaxed his face to correct its asymmetry, but something was distracting him. At first it was a vague sensation, then an unpleasantness directly under his nose, until finally a palpable stench of burning mixed with wafts of a fetid acidity besieged him. Gulping down the saliva lodged in his throat, he looked around him: the walls were half-destroyed and black with soot and the wooden windowsills had been burnt to a cinder. He had heard about the violence of the conquest of Solsona but, as usual, it had never occurred to him that those words had anything to do with reality. Battle reports would filter through to him but he would not give the dead a moment's thought until the bodies were laid out before him. Likewise, they could sing the praises of some new chef until they were red in the face but for him the proof was always in the pudding. He regretted being so oblivious. Living surrounded by grandiloquent speeches on the perpetuity of the world, he amused himself with them, happy to be the cornerstone of all those verbal castles. Were it not for the pleasure of listening to those transfiguring words he would have packed the adventure in a long time ago. Nevertheless, each time one of those words manifested itself he felt a dull ache in his stomach. He was brooding gloomily over it all when a noise jolted him out of his reverie. It was the crowd, packed into the gateway like sardines, cheering him on vehemently. Don Charles stretched his lips into something resembling a smile before the mayor offered him his rod, which he magnanimously rejected. When a group of councillors tried to cover him with a canopy, his horse startled and the monarch sent them scurrying with a quick, brusque flick of his hand.

Inside the city walls the stench became denser. Mangled houses came into view, openly displaying their rotting entrails and broken bones. The king, dripping with sweat under his uniform, had since dismounted and was focussing on the fervent greetings coming from both sides of the street by bare-chested men, and women wrapped in black shawls. They adored him without even knowing him; they adored him to such an extent that they didn't think twice about defiling themselves with hatred for their adversaries. Amid the commotion, a cry could be heard growing in sound and assertiveness, until it finally exploded ecstatically through the crowd like buckshot from the soldier's blunderbusses: "Death to Christina the Whore!" The king re-examined the faces in the crowd, shining next to the blackened walls. Turning to the councillor closest to him, much too close for his liking, he quietly remarked: "This displeases me greatly and makes me most uncomfortable." He made an appeasing motion with his hand but the noise continued. He looked at the mob again, his eyes now hopelessly asymmetric. To his right, a man as strong as an ox had a tiny boy with large, protruding ears clinging to his neck. The brat was shouting "kwistinawhore, kwistinawhore" and laughing maniacally. His face was even more asymmetric than the king's.

Don Charles Maria Isidre de Borbó felt lightheaded. The masses, the clamour, the royal fanfare all seemed excessive to him and he was having a hard time staying upright. Just as his body began to teeter dangerously, a tall, wiry foreign soldier walking in front of him turned, as if propelled by providence, and took command of the situation. The king's eyelids were drooping, his mouth hung partially open in a gormless smile and his back was hunched over. The soldier, terrified about the consequences of a royal decline and fall in the middle of all those delirious displays of devotion, and with a level of resolve unbeknown even to him, stomped on the imperial foot. A loud shriek rang out. His eyes opened, his mouth closed and his back straightened. Once again, the king puffed out his chest and paraded with aplomb. The red-faced soldier hung his head in dismay.

All the members of the city council and the Supreme Royal Governing Junta of the Principality of Catalonia were in position behind the monarch. Halfway along Llobera Street, the procession met the one presided over by the bishops of Solsona, Lleida and Mondoñedo coming from the cathedral. Throne and altar now united, they advanced in unison towards the temple before taking their seats in the chancel.

The choir began to intone a *Te Deum* as, half-illuminated by the light cast by the stained glass windows of the apse, the king settled into contemplation. The cathedral was tall, long and crooked, and the pews were packed with people, but about four or five rows back he saw a head tower momentarily above the others. The choir reminded all present that heaven and earth, the seraphim and cherubim, and the great celestial powers praised the Lord. Don Charles was moved and dreamt (though somewhat shocked by the splendour of the dream, he strained to situate his desire within the sad, ephemeral limits of human existence) about the day he would enter Madrid and each of those measly little Spaniards would worship him without exception, having rejected the enchantments of new and confusing doctrines. The king gazed up at the arches; it was a fine cathedral, despite its crookedness. He then caught sight again of a reddish head raised above the others and felt a pain in his foot.

Surrounded by a swarm of high-ranking officials, Don Charles exited the cathedral and was led to the Episcopal Palace where he was to spend the night, the bishop having put his personal living quarters at his disposal. With the monarch and young prince now seated in the reception area, the hand-kissing could get under way. The city councillors, the members of the Supreme Royal Junta, the bishops and generals, the idle yet inquisitorial marquises, the awkward priors and the Mothers Superior all filed ceremoniously past before a fleeting image startled the king out of his stupor: that same narrow, angular, reddish head appeared from behind a curtain. It was only there for a second; perhaps it was fatigue playing tricks on him.

After the hand-kissing ceremony, it was time to step out onto the balcony to watch the Catalan troops parading. There were more than ten thousand soldiers. How long would it take: one hour? Two, perhaps? Standing with his hands gripping the balustrade, he felt a persistent, penetrating pain in his foot, much like the existence of the Liberals. The troops were advancing far too slowly. As the king turned towards his nephew to make the conventional extolment of proceedings, he shuddered: standing behind him was that strange foreigner, a full foot taller, looking down at him with a smile smeared across his emaciated face.

'Keep this man as far from my royal person as possible,' uttered Don Charles to the first minister to hand.

The man's name was Rudolf von Wielemann and he had

crossed a score of German principalities, the entire kingdom of France, the Pyrenees, the Principality of Andorra, more Pyrenees, the Pre-Pyrenees, hills, canyons, highlands and plains with the intention of joining the royal expedition that newspapers across Europe were talking about. As he followed the River Segre, he paid keen attention to the rumours situating the sovereign slightly further south. As soon as he arrived in Biosca, he learnt that the royal retinue had departed in the direction of the Sanctuary of the Holy Miracle, south of Solsona. The morning sun was already glistening among the trees when he spurred his horse on, bracing himself for one final push.

Clutching a letter of recommendation from his uncle, Gottfried von Wielemann, general in the Prussian army, Wielemann made several unsuccessful attempts to present it and thus enlist in the Carlist forces in a proper yet not too perilous position.

His Majesty's ministers were hurriedly (or at least they made it look like they were) preparing the monarch's entrance into the capital of Catalan Carlism and the commanding general of the armed forces, Blas María Royo, was either absent or unavailable. The senior officers he had attempted to speak to ran their eyes over the letter with an air of interest, said that it was written in the language of Napoleon and maintained their interested look a little while longer before bowing quickly and bidding the foreigner farewell with a self-satisfied "*très bien*", "*bien*", "*molto bene*" or "*bravo*". It didn't seem like anyone was willing to give any orders.

Wielemann wandered through the grounds of the sanctuary. Next to an entrance built of old, dark stone, the roofless pillars and arches held themselves aloft among the nettles and weeds, surrounded by an assortment of discarded rocks. It was nothing more than a half-finished, abandoned building but there was something alarmingly apocalyptic about it. He went into the empty church; all the pews had been removed and the filthy floor was covered with straw all the way up to the Baroque altarpiece where golden figures and ornaments shone in one gleaming, glorious mess. Four peasant women were knelt in prayer in front of the altar. Wielemann left them to it and set about studying the dozens of panel paintings covering the opposite wall. His eyes skipped over the figures' anaemic faces. A rock had crushed a man and three others were trying to save him. A gang of individuals were threatening a young man with their bayonets. Two men in traditional Catalan dress, brandishing their rifles, were grinning next to a bloody corpse. Five daughters and two sons were keeping vigil over their dying father, while the priest got ready to perform the last rites. Outside, Death – a faceless being with soft, white flesh, wrapped in a cape (or was it an enormous wing?), neither plant nor animal – was waiting. The mortally wounded, the shipwrecked, the condemned – all were saved at the last moment. The Virgin Mary who kept watch over them was triangular and cross-eyed. Exactly what sort of worship could possibly be satisfied by these parodies of pathos? On the left-hand panel of one triptych, a woman could be seen offering up prayers to a schematic Christ figure, while on the right, inside a house, there was a man stripped naked, with nothing but a sheet covering his nether regions, as two moustachioed surgeons stood over him. One of the surgeons was bringing a butcher's knife towards the man's head and the reason for the horror in his eyes, mere sketches but crystal clear, and the desperation in his arms, trusting all to God, became apparent. Wielemann bit his lip. A second later the man's skull would have been oozing blood. How deep did that so-called doctor want to perforate? And what miracle was being praised here? The fact the Virgin Mary had liberated the man from his illness? Or that she had rescued him from the doctor? As usually happened when told of or witness to some agonizing scene, Wielemann felt a sharp pain in the place he imagined the wound to be. When he turned to leave he saw, standing so close to him that he was almost breathing down his neck, a dishevelled individual with greasy hair and a moronic grin who looked as if he had been carefully extracted from one of those panels with a pair of tweezers. Wielemann interrogated him with his stare but the smile was unbreakable. He pushed the individual out of his way like one might part the undergrowth and went outside.

Everywhere there were groups of ragged soldiers drinking, smoking, and socking each other by surprise. One of these groups shouted something Wielemann's way and he didn't have the courage to ignore them. Amused by his appearance, they asked him questions he didn't understand but which he assumed were concerning his origin.

'*Je suis allemande de Prrrussie. Prrrussien. Prusse.*'

'*Russe?* Russian, you say?'

Wielemann's face was the picture of concentration.

'They Catholics in Russia?'

'You betcha.'

'Carlists?'

'I guess so'

'Strange.'

'I wouldn't trust him if I was you. Who knows what he's hiding.'

Like a stuffed gorilla in a natural history museum, Wielemann found himself plumb in the middle of six men eyeing him with interest while moving slowly around him. One of them was a massive fellow with a pale face and swollen cheeks, lurching from side to side as though he were too heavy for his own legs, wearing a smile that said: "ain't nobody gonna pull the wool over *my* eyes". Next to him was a tall, olive-skinned man who rolled his Rs heavily and whose smile was difficult to distinguish from a confused or a concentrated scowl. The other four were all equally as short but of contrasting widths: the first was a chubby blonde chap who occasionally emitted a mechanical laugh that erupted out of the abyss before abruptly plunging back into it without warning; the second, not quite as chubby as the first, twitched his leg incessantly while his head, home to a few remaining ginger hairs, would fill with ideas until boiling point before his booming voice would echo across the entire esplanade; the third, of average width, was soft-spoken and discreet in a way that was out of tune with the others and when he had something to say they all had to keep quiet and concentrate in order to follow him. The last of the group wasn't just gawky, ghostly white and with the look of being permanently in a trance but – unheard of for a so-called guerrilla – wore thick steam-filled spectacles full of dark splodges and impenetrable muck. These were the Shambolic Six and their dissonant, communal laughter, deep, monotonous and varied like the voices of the forest, encircled Wielemann. Without warning, a painful grimace came over the gawky individual's face and his hands shot up to cover his ears:

'No, no, I'm going deaf!'

'Oh, you're kidding me. Not now...'

'Oh, Our Lady of the Miracle! Our Lady of the Cloister! The wheel is stopping!'

'Don't be alarmed, mister. This one sometimes gets it in his head that he hears strange noises. He says he hears a creaking wheel, that it's creaking in his ears and he can't hear nuffin' else, and then he starts doing circles with his head and he goes all red like a tomato and swings his arms round like he's got to turn some big wheel all on his own. He gets terrified everything'll stop if he don't do nuffin' about it. He says it's the wheel of time. Then he runs up and down bawling his head off and chomping his teeth and bashing into the walls. After, he starts blubbering like a bleeding baby and runs away. Sometimes he flaps his arms like he's a bird trying to take off and then he hurls himself through the air and gives himself a right good whack! The whole time he says stuff like...'

'What are you doing? You fools! Can't you hear the crashing wheel of time? Don't you understand it'll stop if you don't help me?'

'See what I mean? The calmer he sees us, the worse he gets. Then he grabs us and tries to drag us off goodness knows where and we give him a good smack round the chops so he leaves us alone and gets busy going off his nut someplace else. And there you have it. The whole thing normally lasts a good couple of hours. He can do ten laps of the church in that time! Then he hits the ground like a sack of potatoes and falls asleep. That's how he got the name Whingebag.'

Whingebag had since run off in zigzags and the sound of his shrieking gradually began to fade into the distance. The chubby one was looking keenly at Wielemann's feet.

'Holy moly, get a load of dem boots.'

'You wouldn't catch me dead in those. They look like they're made of gypsum. This one's got one foot in the grave already, if you ask me.'

'He ain't killed as much as a fly in his whole life.'

'P'raps that's how Russians are s'posed to look. One time, on the road to Manresa, I saw this foreign bloke who looked like a ghost.'

Je viens pour lutter à côté de Sa Majesté le roi don Carlos.

'Oi, oi! Long live Charles the Fif!'

'And the Spanish Inquisition!'

'Death to Christina the Whore!'

'Long live Golferics, the dirty slag!'

'Who's that?'

'Someone I know with a big pair.'

'P'raps she knows someone with a small pair.'

'Oi, come here, you son of a bitch!'

The two chubby Carlists squared up to one another, much to the amusement of the tall Carlists and to the concern of the Carlist of average width. Taking advantage of this new round of thumping, Wielemann crept away, heading off to gaze at the pond next to the church courtyard. It was already getting dark. A stone cross rippled across the surface of the water; beside it swam silent, distant, frugal fish.

Letting fate run its course, the following morning Wiele-mann was among the expedition as it departed for Solsona. Careful not to draw too much attention to himself, he tried to move in circles around the royal escort in order to avoid any possibility of an extended conversation or angst-ridden, rambling exchange. After the frustrated attempts of the previous day, he was wary of words he didn't understand or know how to say. There would be plenty of time to come to a gentlemanly agreement with someone; now it was all about being there, adjusting to his new surroundings and not getting left behind. When they arrived in Solsona, the king, inspiring his utmost respect, was walking immediately behind him. It pained Wielemann to see him so exhausted and he didn't hesitate to rush to his aid when he saw him on the verge of fainting.

Once inside the city walls, he did everything he could to stay close to the monarch. All around him were the people who could be of most assistance. He had attended the church service, he had endured the drawn out and tuneless *Te Deum*, he had even withstood the endless hand-kissing. Finally, when he was standing closer than ever to the king, a royal aide demanded that he accompany him and he thought the moment to make his mark had arrived at long last. But that gruff, bearded man seemed unwilling to listen. He hastily introduced himself but Wielemann wasn't able to catch his name. They crossed the Plaça del Bisbe, brimming with soldiers and rumourmongers, and cut through the Plaça Major, where bands of guerrillas and excited residents were jostling up and down. Afterwards, they turned up a narrow street and headed towards a sloping square with a chapel in the middle surrounded by fountains, whereupon the stench – by now familiar to Wielemann – acquired a few additional ingredients. The man left him in front of the doorway to a large, aristocratic house. Marking each syllable and pointing his index finger and threatening eyes at him, he slowly said:

'You are to help here. Here. Hospital. Help. You. Got it? Order of His Majesty.'

The large foyer was full of bodies spread out upon a smattering of straw. There were legs severed above the knee, arms missing hands, hands missing fingers, and long scars could be seen traced across some of the bare chests while others displayed an ensemble of wounds and sores like extravagant arabesques. The patients' faces swung between despair and the joy at having escaped the clutches of death. Three nuns glided as light as a feather between the men, a *porró* in one hand and a small cloth in the other. When they knelt down the injured men would open their mouths to receive the thin jet of red wine that spurted from the spout before allowing their lips to be patted dry and looking at their benefactors with ambiguous gratitude and a saintly glow in their eyes. Wielemann didn't dare distract the nuns from their work and even less so strike up conversation with any of the convalescents; he was scared to interfere with the mysterious order of that scene unfolding before him like a carefully rehearsed play demanding silence and stillness from its public. A single chair propped up against the wall seemed the perfect invitation. Once seated, Wielemann felt the full force of the sweat and fatigue of the previous weeks. It was still less than a month ago when, at home in Berlin, his father reminded him that at ("how old are you now?") twenty-seven years old a Wielemann was expected to have done something significant in life and that this expedition of Spanish legitimists, object of admiration and sentimental flights of fancy among Europeans of good standing, was a golden opportunity to make a name for himself in Prussia, perhaps even to secure a comfortable position in the government or army. Sure, the inhabitants of the Iberian Peninsula could hardly be relied upon for much, but one should never question the incorrupt nobility of primitive peoples. A relative who had visited Spain forty years earlier noted in his diary that stepping foot in Madrid was like going back in time two hundred years. The map of Europe, in addition to providing a geographical representation of the continent, also traced the passage of time. Prussia was the future of order; France, the confusion of the present; Spain, a rustic and charming past, full of pious women and simple-hearted men who still fought wars in the old style. While listening to these pronouncements, Wielemann asked himself what on earth any of that had to do with what the newspapers were printing about the Carlist guerrillas. The Spanish, continued his father, had fought most heroically against Napoleon and there was no doubt that once the war was over, the country would return to its otherwise permanent state of being: serene, harmless and with as much romanticism as a mist-laden ruin under the light of a full moon. With a letter of recommendation from Uncle Gottfried, Don Charles de Borbó would be sure to receive him personally and with open arms. He would ask him to write it first thing in the morning. Why, he could leave that very week! A year later, safely back at home with a military medal pinned to his chest, he would bring honour to the family and his future would be assured.

The nuns were nowhere to be seen. A few of the convalescents spied Wielemann with curiosity and tried to ask him something. He responded with a phoney smile and the men seemed disappointed. He had understood he was there to help but he didn't know what he was supposed to be helping with. Low but decisive voices filtered down from upstairs and he stood up and began to climb the staircase. In one of the rooms there was a spindly nun, two burly men, and a shorter man. A drowsy-looking soldier was spread out on a bed, his eyes half-closed. Wielemann approached the door one slow step at a time but no one paid him the least attention. The short man gave a brief order and then began putting on a mask, a pair of glasses and a surgical cap, before picking up a butcher's knife. The two burly men clamped the soldier's arms and legs down. The knife sank into the flesh, it sawed into the bone and screams filled the building. A pool of blood spread across the floor. Wielemann stepped backwards and leant against the wall next to the stairs and his head drifted off far away, beyond the Pyrenees, along the back roads of Europe, over the principalities of Germany, before returning to brood among the shadows of the Church of the Holy Miracle, the grotesque paintings, and the roofless, pointless pillars. He then launched himself headfirst into a pond of black blood, sank to the bottom, lost consciousness, and proceeded to tumble down the stairs like a ton of bricks.

3

It was impossible not to notice the derelict two-storey house amid the palaces along Unter den Linden, its windows covered with scraps of paper, its ramshackle roof and discoloured walls, the ground floor barely poking its head above the lowest windows of the two towering buildings it was wedged between. It was as though someone had pressed the house down into the ground. The path leading from the pavement to the front door was hidden under a thick layer of mud and dead leaves. The sheer desolation of it fascinated him. He couldn't tear his eyes away from it. He knelt down on the nearest bench, which was facing the opposite side of the avenue - 'This way, over 'ere! Ah, it's only a bump!' - placed his arms on the backrest and, maintaining that ridiculous lobster pose, scrutinised each dead window a long while, waiting for some sign of life. He felt the building's magnetism and he recalled the vague stories he had been told about a depressed countess. As he approached the house, he saw in the first-floor window furthest to the right, through an uncovered rectangular gap, a pale hand with long fingers wearing a diamond ring and moving as if caressing a round object. It was the hand of a prisoner, he was sure of it, locked away in that house by some depraved individual who had cut themselves off from - 'There're no more houses left. Take him to the widow's place.' - the world and who ruled his dominion with an iron fist. It was a hand in need of a saviour. He felt the saliva move up and down in his throat, waiting to be gulped down. What was he willing to risk for that creature full of grace? But the hand had vanished. He scrutinised each window again but, alas, he saw no hand, no tiny finger. The building had returned to its previous lifelessness. He was tired and ready to leave when he saw an old man dressed in brown clothes walk through the open door, rummage inside a cubbyhole, begin to go down the stairs, turn back and close the door before (and he was certain of it) descending the staircase again towards a basement room where he kept every kind of torture instrument imaginable. His hands beginning to tremble, he prayed for it all to stop, or at least that the old man become incapacitated somehow so that he might throw himself upon him. Then he thought about those long, slender fingers and watched himself break down the door to the blind house, race down the stairs and, there, in the middle of the torture chamber…

When Rudolf von Wielemann awoke from his unsettling dream he found himself lying in a damp, unfamiliar bed in a small room with filthy white walls and a crucifix above the door. His head was pounding. Groping the back of his neck he discovered an ostentatious lump apparently connected to the nerves in all four limbs which transformed itself into a tight, painful knot when he tried to sit upright. Walking a few steps, he leant against the doorframe and saw a dimly lit room with a staircase leading upwards, a table, a painting on the wall, and a casement window looking out onto an unharvested field. Sat facing the only source of natural light was a woman shelling fava beans. She had white, almost velvety hair, which spread across her shoulders and down her back, and thin, fast-moving fingers that made the beans fall like hail into a pot full of water. When a pod took exception to being ripped apart, she raised her arms, stretched them, listened for a damp snap and then recaptured her rhythm. Wielemann took a step forward and the woman turned and looked at him impassively. Though her hair was white, she must have been around forty – ten or fifteen years older than him – and her face, despite the detachment it sought to transmit, appeared tender and vivid. Her eyes, however, were the most remote part of her, burning like two beacons on a mountain ridge, visible for miles and miles in the depths of a winter night, perhaps only sensed, perhaps mere figments of the imagination.

The woman said something Wielemann didn't understand

before disappearing into the kitchen and returning with a plate of mashed potatoes mixed with bits of bacon. After leaving it on the table she went to stand by the wall and contemplated her guest with a blank gaze that might have concealed curiosity, desolation or indifference: it was impossible to know. Wielemann summoned the strength to walk a few steps, sit down and drag his chair under the table. He ate the potato, cabbage and bacon slowly, aware only now of the emptiness in his stomach. Looking over again at the figure beside the wall, he then proceeded to eat more potato, more cabbage, more bacon, all the while savouring the revitalising taste of the meat on the tip of his tongue. He scraped the plate clean and the woman filled it again. He ate more quickly, more impatiently now, noting the anxiety grow in his chest. She served him more. Wielemann wolfed the food down with a prehistoric hunger, like a predatory animal, with a velocity that obliged him to have his mouth full at all times and to be constantly forcing the food down his gullet. Occasionally he struck the table with his fist in order to regain his self-control and shot a secret, ashamed look over at the face framed by a halo of white hair. He satiated his body as if physical satisfaction were not nearly enough.

By the time it was dark the woman had disappeared into some other part of the house. Wielemann sat alone by the window. In pain from head to toe, he allowed his mind to wander. Soldiers were ambling up and down the street between the house and the open field, singing, shouting slogans and belching. Wielemann's memory of that morning, the royal entry and his visit to the makeshift hospital was foggy at best. He couldn't be sure exactly what had happened, but he assumed they had put him in that forlorn place because whatever buildings had not burnt to the ground were now occupied by the king's thirty thousand soldiers. He decided it was too late to venture outside. Anyhow, the expedition would be in the city for a few more days. He patted his chest in order to hear the rustle of his uncle's letter, his lifeboat amid that foreign sea. He then patted some more, in complete confusion.

The letter was missing.

Going back into the bedroom, he rummaged in his bag, his coat, the bedside table, the sheets, shelves, and shadows under the bed.

The letter wasn't there.

In those days the city presented two irreconcilable images. The buildings were either half destroyed or had been left inaccessible by tonnes of teetering stone. The most fortunate beams had got away with being scorched, the rest lay snapped in two or smashed to smithereens. These were the remains of the battle between the Liberals and the Carlists some two months prior. The former, fleeing *en masse* with entire families, burnt everything they could. Yet through this landscape, upon which it seemed some god had unleashed their unbridled wrath, uniformed officers, immaculately dressed aristocrats and cheerful clergymen were casually strolling. They had appeared from who knows where and were exhibiting themselves with the responsibility of those representing an entire world, a world temporarily exiled but preparing for its gliding descent back to earth. Wielemann was then forced to cross paths with a short and stocky man with a blue cap half covering his shaved scalp, a sabre and two musketoons dangling from his belt, who was walking through the city with a wounded horse trailing behind him. They had just made him a captain and he was parading with a permanent half smile and flushed cheeks, engulfed by the stench of anisette. The highest-ranking officers hated and feared him in the same breath, whereas the general populace, despite enjoying the odd laugh at his expense, were full of admiration because they saw in him a man who was brutal and quotidian in equal measure, a man who revealed just how much brutality everyday things are made of. This was the Reverend Father Benet Tristany, lover of Catholic pomp, summary executions, and that territory's rugged terrain, and no doubt Wielemann had never laid eyes on anyone quite like him, so unyielding, so untouched by complicated thought. First and foremost, Tristany did things his way: he was like sentences formed by those who have never learnt any grammar. Despite having attended seminary school he wasn't waging war out of loyalty to any particular doctrine. He did it for the same reason wolves devour sheep: out of the certainty of instinct.

Among the groups walking up and down the main street, he also repeatedly saw the bearded man who had dumped him at the makeshift hospital by order of the king. Wielemann watched him with wide eyes and a nascent smile on his lips, nodding his head, hopeful of obtaining a serious post. The man, clearly ill at ease, looked the other way.

The days passed and the officers became increasingly few and far between. The soldiers had all but disappeared. The royal expedition was preparing to march again. Wielemann was desperate to follow but had no idea where to begin. Blurred images of his arrival appeared to him, accompanied by stabbing pains. He was unable to locate his horse or remember who he had entrusted it to; if, of course, he had entrusted it to anyone. Everywhere people were talking in hushed yet hurried tones, with restrained excitement, about imaginary and improbable plans. The king was departing, perhaps for Barcelona or, even better, for Madrid. Mouths were already beginning to drool, as though an enormous meal were in the offing followed by the sustained stillness of an afternoon nap.

Wielemann searched high and low, or at least he pretended to, even if it were merely to maintain a sense of self-respect. When he approached men who seemed to be in the know he would seize up due to the pain in his back and for fear of not finding the right words, of not understanding their reply, of remaining trapped between languages.

Wandering aimlessly, he turned a corner and almost crashed head on with the man who could make decisions on behalf of the king, the bearded official from the first day. They both stopped dead in their tracks and the man, turning his shoulder slightly, made to walk away. This was Wielemann's last chance. The soldiers were already filing past in formation and the man would be gone in next to no time. From the depths of his memory, Wielemann senior appeared, his forefinger raised, and chastised him. Making a monumental effort, channelling the energy of his forefathers, Wielemann junior stepped suddenly to his left and blocked the bearded official's path. The man was left perplexed and could do nothing more than turn the other way. With the joy at feeling his strength renewed, Wielemann triumphantly intercepted him again. The man took a step back and visibly bristled.

'*Aidez-moi, monsieur. Je suis ici pour lutter à côté du roi. J'avais une letter de mon oncle, mais…*'

'You are to stay in Solsona. *Restez ici.* Special mission. Order of His Majesty.'

And with that, he disappeared. Wielemann turned around. Standing behind him and observing him closely was a man he recognised from the king's entrance, someone he seemed to remember being among the city councillors. He was tall, shaped liked a carpenter's brace and had a round nose the colour of a ripe tomato. The man had heard the words "special mission" and seemed intrigued.

'Foreign friend, have you come to defend cross and crown? Come and eat with me. *Comer. Menjar. Manger. Chez moi. Je m'appelle* Joseph Soler. It would be an honour. *Demain.* Plaça Major.'

He then grasped Wielemann's hand and shook it frenetically with a movement not just of the arm but of his entire body, brimming with anticipation, and then left with the air of someone with a tremendous amount to do. For the first time since he had crossed the Pyrenees, Wielemann had understood two conversations in a row. Now, however, he wanted nothing more but for the ground to swallow him up.

4

Between the pages on Wielemann, responsibility dictates I must translate, at least a bit.

When it came to writing, Prince Lichnowsky had no time for verbose or ornate prose, rather making his words fall in with the style of a competent commander: sure, efficient, exact. Given the importance he placed on calling things by their name, his book is as free from lyrical outpourings as his life was. Nevertheless, on the few occasions he did feel inclined to poetry, he drew on his military resolve, always knowing where to draw the line.

In June 1837, the prince was part of the royal expedition that left both Solsona and Wielemann behind. He followed the Cardener downriver to Súria and then travelled onward to Sant Fruitós. Father Tristany was at the siege of Santpedor and it was there that one of his famous cannon backfired, taking a few of the chief engineer's fingers with it. Afterwards, Lichnowsky watched the breaking dawn with foreigner's eyes, refusing to reduce the world to a simple representation:

We lifted the siege of Santpedor and commenced our retreat towards Súria, whence we departed on the 24th at four o'clock in the morning, passing in silence over the topmost summit. Montserrat, Cardona, the open plain and its countless villages, the sea and, far into the distance, on the edge of the horizon, the tiny black dot of Mallorca: like a vast living map, all that was spread before us; but we were too mindful of the significance of that decisive march to permit ourselves the pleasure of contemplating that image [...].

5

In July, just a few days after the conquest of Berga, the Supreme Royal Governing Junta and the last of the Carlist celebrities abandoned Solsona. It could be said that the city returned to its customary calm, but that would not be wholly accurate, for it was a new calm, made up of toppled walls, ossified ideas and wounded men. The streets offered Wielemann nothing but silence and stares. Now there were no more foreigners left, he felt more conspicuous than ever when he crossed paths with a local. His gut feeling was that he had no business being there and that his presence made no sense whatsoever, but that sensation was superseded by a much more powerful one, nurtured for years from a tender age: orders were to be taken seriously. Though merely verbal, he had received a clear and precise command. Special mission: don't budge from this town. He assumed they would send him more details before long. It was admittedly all very strange, but then he was in a foreign country, after all. Traipsing the solitary streets, he pondered how receiving an order that, for the time being, didn't require him to do anything or, rather, required him to do nothing, wasn't a situation altogether different from the lethargic life he had maintained his entire adult existence in Berlin. A day might start with the reading of some fanciful story or philosophico-religious digression, after which he would play a sonata, then poke his head out the window and spy some girl walking along the avenue with whom he would fall madly in love before falling out of love over lunch. Later, he might pretend to work on some assignment sympathetically bestowed upon him by Uncle Gottfried, read a little more and generally partake of the pleasure of not producing anything. There were days, however, when he felt thoroughly accompanied in his in-activity: when his cousin Caroline visited with her parents and it was mandatory to listen to her play the piano. On one such day, Mr and Mrs Wielemann sat politely in their respective arm-chairs while the girl's parents held hands on the sofa. Rudolf had placed himself between the two couples with his back hunched over, stifling a smile. Caroline, perched straight as an arrow, looked at the piano keys, rocked backwards and then attacked. A simple sonata with a childlike quality began: Beethoven's Op.49 No.1. Caroline bumped along like an old cart, rearing up and plunging her full weight down onto the piano whenever a *forte* approached, making the notes ring out like smashing glass. The bars came and went with considerable difficulty, as though embarrassed to form part of that succession of disasters. The movement concluded and Caroline turned to receive the approving gaze of her parents and the stiff politeness of the Wielemanns. Rudolf amused himself by observing the blond curls skip along the back of her neck with its porcelain skin and fine hairs, a neck that seemed made to be held, silky skin that seemed made to be caressed. A spark of electricity ran through his body. It was a tender, nostalgic little piece of music, with only a couple of bars hinting at the composer's heroic impetus, that cry of humanity in love with itself and which desires to be stronger, freer and more fraternal. But Caroline played those two bars like someone struggling with a rusty lock. The ideal limped along, stumbled, fell in the mud, managed to drag itself to its knees after some fortuitous syncopation and then continued to crawl on all fours, completely crushed under his dear cousin's fingers. Oh, how heartwarming, yet pathetic, familiar things are! Walking along the streets of Solsona, Wielemann had the same subdued smile on his lips, he could hear that jolting music once again and feel the electricity under his shirt. The development had finished and the recapitulation was now beginning, the left hand stumbled as always, but in a different, unexpected manner.

In an unexpected manner? Wielemann looked up. The music really was being played: it existed outside of his head. The notes from Op.49 No.1 were coming from a window in that godforsaken town wedged into the southern foothills of the Pyrenees. Wielemann located the front door to the house in a gloomy, narrow side street and pushed it open. There were a number of steps, all of them eroded and uneven. The sonata was getting closer. At the top of the stairs on the right, there was a dark room where an enormous pot boiled over a fire watched over by a wide, weary-looking old woman, both as motionless as objects in a diorama. The music was coming from the left. In a spacious room with two windows, a bookshelf, armchairs and a wall clock, a small man was playing a square piano. He played with passionate movements, as though each note electrocuted him, but the music was rotten. The more exaggerated the gesture, the more grotesque the sound, in a way that reminded one of those little music boxes that so captivate children and simpletons. The sonata ended with a jolt and the small man turned around looking surprised. He had a familiar air about him.

'*Vous êtes tombé il y a quelques jours, n'est-ce pas?*'

Wielemann didn't remember if he had fallen or not, but he now recognised the man sitting there. He appeared before him clutching a butcher's knife and he recalled a terrifying scream and a drop of black blood spreading out until it covered everything, and then the empty, dimly-lit room where he had woken up. Despite the deep lines on his forehead, the doctor didn't seem much older than Wielemann. Now, without the pincers or those blood-soaked overalls, and with his courteous, interested gaze, anyone would have taken him for someone else entirely.

'*Vous êtes le messieur russe, n'est-ce pas?*'

'*Je suis prussien, messieur, pas russe.*'

'*Je jouais Beethoven,*' replied the doctor, his eyes opening a little wider.

'*Je le sais. Est-ce que vous me permettez de jouer?*'

What happened next is difficult to evoke with words and impossible to restore to life, but if I don't at least try I fear Wielemann's story will fall on deaf ears. First and foremost, bear in mind that in those days – given sound recording didn't exist – all music was a fleeting and unrepeatable experience and each performance an irreplaceable gift. Afterwards, infuse each of my words with the intimate memory of some discovery, of some slice of your life that seemed abounding with fulfilled promises and unexpected prophecies. Thus, perhaps these pages will not remain completely silent. Almost imperceptible at the beginning, a deep progression of repeated chords rose up with short melodic phrases gliding occasionally above them. It was an unusual progression that passed from the plenitude of the major mode to a hasty melancholy in minor mode. The music grew and the melody began to soar, transforming into *roulades* until it reached a *forte*, whereupon everything softened and paused on the tonic, now fragile and hesitant. The doctor, sitting in one of the armchairs, held his breath and leant forwards slightly. The same phrase began again, only louder and higher, and another row of frenetic quavers raced off before coming to a *forte* and three *sforzandi*. The melody descended in leaps, in *staccato*, modulating in a way the doctor had never heard before until flowing into a choral, placid, peaceful theme, like a sunlit afternoon in the mountains. He raised his head, filled his lungs, opened his eyes and it was like climbing a rocky path lined with plants that wrap around one's ankles and seeing a sweeping plateau with tiny groups of people stretched out amid the lush green, recovering after some natural disaster with the gratitude of survivors, forgetting everything, being born again into a brave new world. He sat more comfortably in the armchair. The notes merged, they multiplied, they hung in mid-air and when he no longer knew what they would do next they returned to the opening chords, now with greater definition, in *pianissimo*, but with all the impetus of youth rushing headfirst into the furore of life and then everything that had already been played was played again, identical but with more accuracy, with implausible precision and he felt it with a frenetic, fearsome inner ecstasy because it seemed so uncontrollable. Then his hands began to travel. He was already acquainted with the chord progression, the arpeggios and the scales surrounding them; now they moved up and down the keyboard, the length and breadth of the world: they skirted the mouths of the deepest, darkest caves, they rose up suddenly towards the sky's cruel clarity, they stretched and curled and drew a dance along the distant horizon, so remote it was unnerving. The surgeon slowly began something resembling a dance with his feet, his fingertips, his head. Now the images were a storm, a sunlit plain, a vociferous multitude, a spring shower, a silent multitude, a dizzying rockface, a long exile, the plateau of survivors, passionate resistance, a vibration of veins and arteries and muscles, an inevitable farewell, the pleasures of friendship, a looming tower, all of it blending into an impossible discordance, yet at the same time all of those images were false and insufficient, as if at the beginning of time the Creator had laid his ideas upon the earth and then swept them away with one movement of his arm and all that remained was the indescribable sound from before the dawning of the world and any image was defamation but that didn't stop them from continuing to appear. The doctor closed his eyes and felt an immense feeling of gratitude. The sound grew in length and intensity, *roulades* appeared above everything, fleeting, inaccessible, but with increasing insistence, until the opening harmony returned like lost innocence and then the same choral song that was like a sunlit afternoon lost amid weeks of stormy weather, yet still it went on, because those repeated chords from the beginning rang out again, more rousing than before, running over the top of one another, coming to a standstill, dissolving into a song of gratitude, a sigh, a final insinuation, the definitive strike of the key. The doctor unclenched his fists, ready to applaud, but didn't have time.

The second movement began with a succession of slow abysses. The doctor's breathing was in cadence with the music. The notes advanced with staggered steps, as if unbalanced by fatigue. There was a purging of images and emotions and everything was of a precise yet uncomplaining poverty. The doctor was motionless again. He no longer thought anything. In fact, he was no longer there because he had fallen into the music and was floating upon it.

The tranquillity, however, was short-lived. With the violent opening of the third movement he once again felt the floor under his feet and began to move them rhythmically in a silent dance. The *rondo*'s recurrent theme carried him away. It was a solid, jubilant melody made up of effusive gestures. His sole feeling now was of unbridled joy and it filled him with the urge to cry out but he contained himself because he knew that if he didn't, it would all be over, yet the more he contained himself the more intense his joy became. He felt a faith in life and humanity that he had never known before, while at the same time sensing every fibre in his body brim with vitality. Everything was one and the same: intellect and flesh, promises and acts, silence and words – the contradictions merged and melted into the last frenetic notes of the *rondo*. And given these concepts and images, words and moments had melted into one, I can no longer relate them, for they are now irretrievably lost to time. The final two chords sounded and the doctor, sitting silently in the armchair, still had time to feel one last tremor ripple through him. In all, it had lasted barely half an hour. The doctor didn't have the words to say what he wanted to say, neither in his language nor in any that the visitor might comprehend. He approached the pianist and stretched out a stiff hand drenched in sweat.

'Miquel Foraster.'

'Rudolf von Wielemann.'

'*C'était quoi, ce que vous jouiez?*'

'Beethoven. *Die Waldstein-Sonate.*'

Wielemann had not played well by any stretch of the imagination. It had been too long since he last practiced and his fingers had become sluggish. He turned to look at the keys and then at the manufacturer's signature: Otter & Kyburz, "Swiss-Germans from Solothurn in Barcelona."

'*Ce piano-ci, une merde...*'

Foraster smiled with an exhalation of breath and became slightly embarrassed about his inner agitation. All at once he had the desire to discuss a whole host of things with the man stood before him, but he was incapable of articulating the feeling of wonder that had possessed him. Nevertheless, his manner of being incapable was already a clear enough confession and Wielemann didn't need anything more to recognise a music lover. A lover who knew little on the subject, who had no doubt not grown up in a musical environment, who perhaps didn't dominate even the rudiments of *solfeggio* and harmony, but who knew how to listen. Foraster asked, like someone paying a compliment, if he was a professional pianist, despite immediately realising that in 1837 no musician worth his salt could possibly end up in Solsona, a burnt out, deserted city where time had long stood still. Wielemann said he wasn't, that he had come from Prussia to fight alongside Don Charles, but when he saw the other man's face he bit his tongue.

'I, for the time being, try to keep Carlists from going to heaven before their time. They don't deserve it. I trust you are feeling better?'

The wall clock struck twelve and a frustrated look descended over Foraster.

'My dear man, unfortunately I must take my leave of you. It's time for my rounds of the wounded.'

They passed the room with the cooking pot and the old woman, both still motionless in the same spot as if having been placed outside of time. Despite the time of day, outside the air felt clean and fresh. Foraster shook Wielemann's hand.

'Make a habit of coming over to play the piano, why don't you?' he said before disappearing.

That afternoon, Wielemann drowsily wandered the streets.

Out of a door emerged three children: a gangly, gaunt girl, a younger girl who imitated the older one's confident stride and a tiny, skeletal boy barely able to walk. The gangly girl had a sack slung over her back that bounced up and down and emitted meows.

The already setting sun still made everything glisten and the three children turned off towards the river. Wielemann followed them.

The tiny boy – two lines of snot streaming from his nose – would stand enraptured before a dead leaf, the foliage of a weeping willow or an indifferent rock and reach his hands slowly forwards. The younger of the two girls would then drag him along by one arm. Occasionally, the same girl would place a hand upon the sack, stroke it carefully and then pull it away sharply as if she had been scratched.

Wielemann viewed them up ahead like some innocent spectacle, by now paying them scant attention. It was a glorious day and the slight hint of a breeze made him feel buoyant. The city vanished, gardens and fields opened up before him and he saw cabins and a lone farmhouse swathed in calm. Wielemann also felt a sense of rapture. In the background he could hear the children's laughter mix with the meowing, stretching like a thin, taut wire. Things were more morose here than in his country, more inexpressive and withdrawn. They didn't bear the weight of so much history and, consequently, caused no distress. Perhaps he had had a stroke of luck. The war didn't seem much like a war. Nobody had to know what he had done during his time with the Carlists but, being a foreigner, he was naïve and ever so slightly irresponsible. It's for this same reason that saints became holier and conquerors more bloodthirsty when they stepped foot in another country. Far from home, our sense of shame lessens its clutch on the reins. The poplar trees passed by, intermittently blocking the shimmering sun. Wielemann found himself by Gorge Fountain, which for some time the residents had decided to call – one dark thing for another – Crow Fountain. The breeze blew stronger. The children were playing with five kittens next to the murmur of the dark water. The little creatures' legs trembled, their meowing vibrated ever more, and the children caressed them with greater affection. Wielemann sat down on a rock. The gaunt girl watched him out of the corner of her eye and muttered a few short words before the younger one whimpered something along the lines of:

'Can't we keep them hidden away somewhere?'

The eldest slowly repeated their mother's instructions and shoved the kittens back in the sack.

It happened in a flash. As luck would have it, the little boy was stood with his back turned, playing with some pebbles. The girl hurled the sack against the fountain wall and the meowing stopped at once. She did it twice more before throwing the kittens behind a bush and tucking the sack under her arm, now dripping with a gooey liquid. The younger of the two girls grabbed hold of the boy's hand and all three set off along the path towards the city with the sun warming their faces.

Wielemann went to look behind the bush.

In the evening, while lying in bed, he wrote in his diary, but his hand was heavy. Endeavouring to jot down his thoughts on the conversation he had had with the doctor, his eyes began to close and his trembling writing began to trail off before stopping altogether. He fell asleep with the pen between his fingers, a drop of ink suspended from the nib and the diary next to his cheek, sleeping liberated from thought, with the pleasant heaviness of days well spent. It was a dreamless sleep, but he was soon torn from his slumber by a strange shrieking. When he poked his head into the adjacent room, all was still. The door to the room occupied by the woman with distant eyes was shut. He lay down again on the bed but he was now sure he could hear a longer, deeper moan, like the cry of a mournful beast. Turning onto his side, he covered his ear with his hand in an attempt to get back to sleep.

6

I intended to go only as far as the newsstand and head straight back home at my usual frantic pace. The bars lining the avenue had yet to set up their outdoor seating and the only people to be seen were those moving mechanically, presumably on their way to work. I walked no less mechanically but with the September breeze rippling through me I felt as spacious and unfettered as a brand-new apartment, having all but forgotten the mundane chapter from Lichnowsky's memoirs waiting for me on my desk. At the newsstand I scanned the ever-predictable headlines of the papers I had no interest in buying, while paying not even the slightest attention to the front page of the paper I had actually left the house for: I merely took it for granted that I would calmly read it later on, even though I often never get around to it. Ritual has a relaxing effect on me.

I was paying when I heard a deep voice say my name. It was R., with his newspaper tucked under his arm and the same sparkle in his eyes he has had ever since retiring from taming teenagers under the pretext of teaching them literature. He wasted no time in telling me he wanted to discuss the Wielemann material I had sent him. I agreed to walk with him as far as his house.

'Perhaps the strangest thing about Wielemann's time in these parts is that it made no sense for him to be here. Apart from the final catastrophe, which I'm not entirely sure can be attributed to his own will, Wielemann didn't do anything. It's not clear why he came here and even less so why he stayed. You have to admit, the story you tell about his arrival is preposterous and his bumping into Don Charles like that is one of the most grotesque and ludicrous things I've ever heard about that ludicrous war.'

'My imagination is ingenuous.'

'So I see, so I see. Don't get me wrong, everything is so absurd that it ends up being fascinating, at least for my devious mind. While the war's staining the fields with blood and the Carlists are busy heading up a cul-de-sac, Wielemann plays the piano, converses, contemplates, strolls, fornicates, gets bored and becomes depressed.'

'A normal life in an abnormal time and place.'

'Or not quite so normal. What I mean is, I'm not sure he stood for anything. I get the feeling Wielemann didn't believe in anything at all. He could only have been driven here by the utopian idea of Order and Legitimacy, but it wasn't necessary for him to experience it up close. Maybe he felt compelled to come here because of a certain atmosphere and nothing else.'

We crossed the bridge over the River Black. R.'s apartment was just around the corner but we were both discussing things with far too much impetus to stop. He looked up and made an impatient gesture with both hands.

'What do you say if we take a little walk by the river?'

The Lichnowsky chapter waiting for me on my desk flashed through my head but before I had time to say yes R. was heading down the steps to the riverbank. We began to follow the water's course.

'But Order and Legitimacy in the north wasn't the same as Order and Legitimacy in the south. Just think about the most typical guerrillas from that rabble. Try to picture Father Tristany, short, filthy and brutish, with a blue cap half covering his shaved scalp, and a sabre and two musketoons dangling from his belt. He'd bring his horse to a halt, dismount and order the soldiers to pray the Rosary. Shabby, scornful men, they smirked but they obeyed. And Tristany smirked back at them. Far away to the left, the Port del Comte mountain range rose up, steep and dark, stirring up bad memories in him. To the right, the hilly landscape of his youth spread like a series of fine tapestries, with its gentle fields and nestling holly oaks, along with the farmhouses with a healthy supply of gossip, good hens, fine pigs, a brooding heir and hearty sausages hung up to dry. While chanting *Ave Maria*, the soldiers – although it's an outrage to use that word to refer to a bunch of men without the slightest notion of order – would picture a maiden full of grace and ask her to pray for them now and at the hour of their death, a death that edged ever nearer like a terrifying lover. With each repetition time slowed and thickened until they reached the *Gloria Patri* and the priest celebrated it by firing into the air. His gunshot blessed the moment, the place, the soldier's blasphemies and the countless revolutionary corpses that would pile up at the next battle. As it was in the beginning, is now, and ever shall be, world without end.'

The last apartment blocks were now behind us. The grass, still moist with the night's cold breath, emitted a mild, caressing aroma. Poplars lined the path on our right and on the left the fields began to open up. R. was gesturing excitedly.

'Just think how those ragged men relished the imagined figure of the Virgin Mary, how they licked their lips fantasising about her, then think about the familiar fragrance of gunpowder and the pleasures of a traditional way of life, pleasures that unite us with childhood friends and divide us forever from those who haven't known the same places. All of that comes before doctrines and ideological get-ups. Sometimes I think that's all the Carlists were: a group of friends defending their collective memories through the use of arms.'

'And it was impossible for those memories to have anything in common with those of some idle Prussian.'

We left behind the last bridge and the main road passing over it. On our right, the metallic-grey sewage works appeared with its pools of foamy, filtered water, surrounded by small and scant-looking trees. We dodged a tractor as it turned down a side path.

'But arms were also a tradition. They say that after the Catalan Revolt of 1640 every subsequent generation of Tristanys rebelled against the established order. I'm not convinced that's exactly how it was, but it does give an idea of what went on in these parts. We left all that behind half a century ago, but violence was the traditional way of life. If the authorities were found wanting then ten men would go out to catch a thief. The authorities were too domineering? Twenty men went out to catch a tax collector. The authorities let their guard down? Then thirty men would set fire to one of the King's buildings. It was a violence that didn't aspire to create anything, let alone cause a revolution; it would simply explode as an instinctive act with each new misgiving, with each new twist and turn of history. The ruling class made every effort to disarm the population, on one occasion even going as far as to prohibit – pointlessly, of course – the possession of knives. Imagine the terror the masses must have caused. Violence…'

'…was their way of intervening in history.'

'Well… That's a phrase that would look good in a book, but it's incorrect. History concerns the ruling class and scholars. Ordinary people, individuals, didn't intervene in history, either because they didn't know what it was or because they didn't give a damn. History imposes order and hierarchy, it subjugates, whereas the traditional violence of the masses was disorderly, it couldn't be controlled: it was like a mysterious and marginalised world which, without warning, would celebrate itself like the arrival of spring.

'And what you're saying isn't merely the concern of scholars?'

R. twisted his head and twitched one corner of his mouth. I immediately felt guilty. It was typical of him to get animated, impassioned, carried away by ideas that seemed more like fantasies, and I couldn't help but cut the ground out from under him. I did it as a kind of reflex, most likely developed as a student when catching the teacher out caused us a pleasure like no other. R. fell silent. The trees began to embrace the path and wrap us in their shade.

7

During the last week of August all of the heat that had been heaped upon the inhabitants of Solsona over the hot summer months, a warmth that was both weighty and, at times, wrathful, erupted into endless rain. From his room, Wielemann could hear nothing but its indifferent, uterine, slightly claustrophobic patter as he read by a flickering candle the gloomy stories from the E.T.A. Hoffman book he had put in his bag back in Berlin. Each corner had its ghost, while each convention, each certainty, its own heavy shadow. When he felt his energy begin to ebb, he would leave his room and sit on the stone window seat and gaze out at the street, the houses and the fields, their image disfigured by the raindrops. The widow appeared only at noon and in the evening to serve his meals and would then vanish without leaving the house. Wielemann had seldom felt so alone while in the company of another person.

The morning the rain stopped a feeling of elation thrust him out into the open air. It was one of those days that made breathing seem more than a mere automatic mechanism. Wielemann inhaled the damp earth, the blackened stubble fields, the satisfying emptiness of the streets, the balconies overhead and the distant, undulating tension of the war.

He held it all inside before slowly exhaling images of the Carlists and the Liberals, the now familiar, friendly faces, the fresh air, the spoilt corn and the soft, nourishing earth.

He had taken the street leading from the Camp Gate down to the Plaça Major. Standing next to the arches were three men gesturing excitedly and a pigeon pecking at the gap between two slabs. Wielemann continued on his way.

'Foreign friend! You remember me? Where you been hiding, huh? I invited you to lunch, remember? Eat, *manger. Chez moi.* Come on!'

Wielemann was trapped by the arm. Resistance was futile. Without knowing exactly how, he found himself sitting at the table in the home of Josep Soler. They had made him sit at one end of the table, facing the individual who had dragged him along. Between them were a silent boy and girl and Soler's wife, who had a face of perpetual fright and whose tiny irises floated in the middle of two milky expanses. Hung on the wall watching over them were faded and distorted prints of saints and a Virgin Mary painted with shabby, lifeless colours.

'Snails, *señor!*'

The man pointed towards the pile of gastropods on a large tray in the middle of the table. While the children began to suck on them furiously, the housewife carefully extracted the innards with a toothpick. Soler signalled to the little girl to serve their foreign guest. With his plate piled high, Wielemann began tapping the shells with his fork as though wishing to see if they would move or if anything might peer out at him.

'This gentleman is Russian and therefore civilised and knowledgeable. *Sagace*. Or is it *savant*? *Je ne sais pas,*' confessed Soler with a tenuous smile.

The man spoke a hotchpotch of words lifted from Royalist newspapers, the aria of some famous opera, school text books and random conversations had around Solsona. The reader will no doubt appreciate it if I refrain from reproducing all of the eccentricities of his speech.

'*Je suis Prussien, señor. Prusiano. Allemand*. Berlin.'

Soler, with a snail in his left hand and a slice of bread in his right, threw his head back as if to get a better look at the man sitting opposite him.

'And what do you make of the war?'

Wielemann arched his eyebrows and gulped down the flesh of a gastropod, immediately detecting a strange movement in his stomach. Soler tapped his fingers on the table while observing him.

'You're a volunteer, ain't you?'

'*Je viens pour lutter à côté de Sa Majesté le roi don Carlos, bien sûr.*'

'Long live Charles the Fif!'

Soler stared sternly at his children until they finally reacted.

'...And the Spanish Inquisition!'

'You see, kids? Thanks to gentlemen like this Russian here, we'll go back to living in peace in no time, and without no damn Liberals. *Muchas gracias, señor.*'

Wielemann would have liked to have been able to stop eating. He pushed a couple of snails to one side of his plate, pretending he had already emptied their shells, but he had the impression that the little girl was watching him out of the corner of her eye. He forced another one down and then realised he needed to relieve himself. Just as he had both palms on the table and was about to stand up, Soler launched into a long lecture.

'This noble city of ours used to be a peaceful place. Yeah, the authorities was all over the place and, sure, there was the odd nasty piece of work knocking about, but Our Lady of the Cloister kept us safe from harm. Ferdinand vii, deep down, was a good sort. Not like that hijacking whore.' He cleared his throat and his wife turned her eyes up as if searching for one of those sorry-looking saints. 'Yeah, Ferdinand was a good sort, but he was surrounded by conspirators who were all desperately waiting for him to die, which they might've sped along a bit n' all, you know what I mean? Now they've multiplied like flies and they're everywhere. They say they all did a runner when we saved the city but that's a lie. A good number of them stuck around and now they hold secret meetings, like the Freemasons they are. But they try to act clever and keep it under wraps. You keep an eye out, sir. You keep a good eye out. They like to pretend they know stuff, but they dirty the good name of science and philosophy and use it to hide their perverted beliefs. You be very careful who you deal with. Look, if you don't mind, I've done a poem that sums it all up to a tee. I spent a whole Sunday on it. They're going to print it in *The Young Observer*. It goes like this.'

Soler cleared his throat again and spat out a small stone before standing up and spreading his arms out. His wife stood to attention with a soldier's unflinching stare and ordered the children to do the same. He then began to solemnly recite.

> For a thousand years
> the Church was free
> from Liberals; can't you see
> the Virgin shedding tears?
> Imagine your daughter,
> or wife, living liberally,
> but it was like literally
> sending pigs to the slaughter.

They all sat down again and Wielemann slumped back into his chair.

'The slaughterer's us, you see? The slaughterhouse is our city. They're the pigs. The simile's a good one, but p'raps it's not completely right. Are they pigs? P'raps. But, then again, p'raps they're more like crows. Crows that bring bad luck. But what I really wanted to explain was how everything got started here. Upstanding Spaniards were all saying the threat of revolution was real. Decent people like us were really put through the mill. You can imagine, huh?'

He then made a decidedly long multilingual aside: '*Vous imaginez. Usted imagina. Voi imagina…* re?… te?' After a quick half smile, he ploughed on.

'Then militia came to our virtuous, Catholic city, all the way from Tarragona. To protect us, they said. And do you know what they did, huh? Well? Do you?!' Soler was starting to get aggressive. After violently slurping on a snail, he threw a fork to the floor, making his wife tremble.

'All day long they lied about, right here, in the Plaça Major, under the arches, just hanging around and carrying out all manner of bodily emissions. Men like me walked past with our heads held high, without looking down for a second. But,' he said, adopting a strident and theatrically high voice, 'those poor priests… oh, those poor things! They crossed themselves when they passed by. And the soldiers, well, they turned around and pulled their pants down! Can you imagine such a thing?' Soler was shouting now. 'Well, can you?! They mooned the priests!'

He was beside himself and remained frozen for a few seconds before repeating the same multilingual aside only this time feebly and hesitatingly: '*Usted imagina. Vous imagine…ez, non? Voi…* ah, sod it…'

'Papa…'

'The priests ran away crying *Ave Maria*. But that's only the half of it, 'cos you'll never guess what they did next!' He wiped the sweat from his forehead before continuing in a soft, velvety voice. 'Me, when I'm out and about, I like to look at the saints up in the niches. I mean, who doesn't? I look at them, say hello, ask them for a favour or two. It helps. I get on best with Saint Paul. He lives a bit further up, behind the town hall. Now, let me tell you this: whenever I'm feeling a bit down in the dumps – which, isn't often, mind – we have a good, long chat and I feel much better for it. This Saint Paul in question has the same face as a childhood friend of mine who died fighting that little stuck-up Frenchy. You know what? We come and we go but the saints, well, they stick around forever.'

'Pa…'

'Wait a sec, sweetheart. One day we was born and one day we'll die. They just watch us passing through. They're the true inhabitants of Solsona, not us. We're just here for a little while before we go to heaven. Hey, we're sort of foreigners, like yourself! You know what I mean? But they know the streets like the back of their hand and they know all the faces too: who's good, who's bad, who they should help, who they shouldn't, and they're up to speed on all the gossip. Right, then…'

Soler got noisily to his feet, screamed at the top of his lungs and thumped a fist up and down on the table, sending the cutlery flying.

'And they went and burnt them! The soldiers burnt the saints!'

He collapsed back into his chair.

'It was heart-breaking to walk past and see all the niches black with soot. My Saint Paul was just a pile of charcoal and didn't speak anymore. I mean, how do you talk to charcoal, anyway? All of a sudden the saints ain't there anymore, and they're s'posed to always be there. Can you imagine the responsibility that came our way? We used to come and go like the flowers and they comforted us, they lasted. And they ain't there no more! Now we last longer than we're meant to and it's us that has to help them. Before, the city could pin its faith on the saints but now it only has us to rely on! But let me tell you this: it didn't stay that way because our Lord and Saviour sent us the glorious guerrilla Tristany to put things straight. Father Benet loves the saints better than no one. He drinks wine straight from the bottle and anything else going. Anyway, turns out one day the same soldiers that burnt the saints were on their way back from Cardona. They were breaking into all the houses with the excuse of looking for Carlists but, thanks to divine providence, the farmers in this county are good folk and they've got good musketoons.'

'But Pa, the man…'

'I said wait a sec. When the soldiers bumped into Father Tristany and his boys, they legged it, naturally, and hid in old Claret's house. It was divine providence, sir! And, listening to divine providence,' he said, his face lighting up, 'Tristany set the place on fire. There must've been fifty of them in there! You could see the smoke from Solsona, a slow, thin line of smoke that looked like it was descending from heaven. When the soldiers tried to escape they were met with gunfire. A few died that way but thirty-six of them didn't even step foot outside; they went directly to hell! Not that they would've noticed the difference, mind. They started burning in this world and continued burning in the next. What a glorious lesson, *n'est-ce pas*? He who burns shall himself be burnt.

'Afterwards, Father Benet liberated our noble city, over five months ago now, and I was offered the lofty responsibility of city councillor. But then these are times of great responsibilities, my man! It's as if the world was falling apart right before our eyes and it was up to us to put it back together again. But it ain't right for men to have to do that. The world was made in the beginning and forever and ever. Well, that's how the theory went, anyhow. And now the world's swarming with destroyers of theory! But luckily for us, not only have we got the Heavenly Father but we also have Father Benet to watch out for us and to hold the heavens up with his bare hands like a kind-hearted giant. We have faith in Don Charles, descendent of His Most Catholic Majesty Philip V, who in two days from now will make his triumphant entrance into Madrid, the axis of Christendom.' Soler cleared his throat again. 'The *axis mundi*, as a man in the know from the University of Cervera told me. The sun of peace shall shine forth once again from Madrid. We have faith in holy providence.'

Soler looked completely spent and was breathing deeply with his eyes half closed.

'Josep, I don't think this man's quite himself. Look at him, he's gone as white as a sheet.'

For some time Wielemann had been feeling an unusual movement in his intestines, as though a band of miniature gnomes were scurrying along them but, between the host's impassioned speech and his own linguistic insecurity, he had not dared open his mouth. As his face grew paler, he desperately searched for a word – any word – that would allow him to

excuse himself. By the time Soler had started on about the puri-
fying fire, the gnomes were already rapidly descending and not
showing any signs of slowing down. Wielemann had begun to
make bizarre movements with his hands, waving them up and
down like a chicken trying to get airborne. Yet had he known
the word, no doubt his sense of shame would have prevented
him from uttering it. It was the little girl who came to his rescue.

'Pa, he wants the toilet.'

After shooting him an examining look, Soler grabbed his
arm again and dragged him down the corridor.

Once alone, the gnomes tumbled downhill, falling over one
another. He breathed a sigh of relief and looked around him. On
the wall a crudely drawn portrait of a king was hanging upside
down and covered in fly droppings, the lopsided handwriting
informing the observer it was Philip v. Wielemann felt another
group of gnomes gathering in his stomach. The man who had
just sung the virtues of the Bourbons had the first Bourbon King
of Spain hanging upside down and engulfed by the stench of
shit. Wielemann remembered his father's words: 'Go to Spain
to re-establish order alongside the legitimists, for they are the
only ones amid the confusion of our days who have coherent and
firm ideas that have stood the test of time. To Spain, to restore
Europe!' Another band of gnomes came plunging down as he
pondered the point of his presence in that war. If it was to obtain
a good – that is to say, uneventful yet steady – position in the
Prussian army which enabled him to devote himself to lying
around and playing the piano all day without anyone getting on
his case about it, then he was willing to suffer to some degree.
If it was to defend the moral integrity of Europe, perhaps it was
worth risking his health, his dignity and the proper functioning
of his intestines, even if merely out of courtesy to his compatriots'
convictions. But no: the war seemed an absurd joke next to his
father's impassioned rhetoric. And there he was, lost in the
middle of it all without anyone to turn to, his guts torn to shreds

and staring at an inverted portrait of Philip v, which could only mean one thing: that these people didn't have the faintest idea of what they wanted and that they would, at the very best, serve as cannon fodder. His head became flooded with images of Prussia. He pictured his pristine piano with its soothing yet solid sound filling the halls with rich resonances while he lost himself amid cascades of disconcerting chords as vast as a forest and melodies that whisked him off to the ends of the earth and beyond. He felt nostalgic for his cousin and longed to hear her destroy Beethoven with that innocent air that always made him overlook her many absurdities. He even missed his father, who was at least far enough away for his ideals to appear endearing.

There was a knock at the door. From his seated position, Wielemann answered with an inquiring tone.

'*Excusez-moi, une petite confusion.*'

Preceded by his tenuous smile, Soler poked his head around the door, reached towards the upside-down portrait of Philip v, unhooked it and tucked it under his arm.

'*Continuez, monsieur, continuez.* I won't be bothering you again.'

8

'I like what you're saying, don't get me wrong, but there's something that doesn't add up to me. Those first Carlists signed up to a plan, they joined the rank and file of a regular army, they put themselves at the beck and call of the most reactionary Bourbon king of all.'

'Not quite. That's what the history books will tell you, yes. But around here, the Carlist War exploded like buckshot. Dozens of cases of spontaneous and badly coordinated acts of violence broke out. The towns and cities were under governmental control, but the woods and back roads belonged to the Carlists. The Royalists, on paper fighting for absolutism and against revolution, weren't subject to any authority. And this scattered violence would land in some town or other, execute a few soldiers, steal arms and supplies, and then disappear back into the woods or over the hills. Barcelona had been stripped bare; almost all its armed forces had been sent to the mountains where they desperately tried to orientate themselves in unknown territory with the help of inaccurate maps and without fully comprehending the pro-Christina soldiers who were supposed to help them. The mounting paperwork of the modern State pitted itself against timeless vulgarities, names carved in stone and anarchic guerrilla units. Fighting for the absolute power of a king, those first Carlists defended a sovereign as remote and paternal as God is to Catholics. Meanwhile, their enemies were being dragged along by the desire to expand the State's bureaucratic apparatus, a desire the history books call – for a reason that is beyond me – Liberalism. It's exactly the same zeal that opposed the Absolute's age-old prerogatives by expelling monks and looting monasteries. Just like when your body's seized by pain and you punch the wall or vomit with a force you've never known before, so the Carlists screamed out with the agonies of modernisation.'

There was hardly any breeze. The sun raged and the pine trees lining the edge of the path cast little, if any, shade. I turned to look at R. He was advancing hurriedly with his eyes fixed on the path ahead and his words interspersed with heavy breathing. The impetus of his ideas seemed to communicate itself directly to his feet because whenever he embarked on an elaborate or expressive explanation, he would accelerate his pace. His intellectual pauses were also physical, and he appeared indifferent to any suggestion I might make. The indignant subject matter likewise filled him with indignation and he was gesticulating like a man possessed.

'A bureaucrat would turn up speaking on behalf of the government or some foreign notary aspiring to control the world with his awful prose. You can well imagine the exasperating effect all that must have had. With the multiplication of laws and regulations, the only thing you understand is you can never be sure they won't screw you over somehow, because the subtleties of the law always favour those who have a monopoly over its interpretation. All you see is them sadistically extending the mechanisms of control and closing private spaces within regulated zones. The paradox, however, is that the expansion of legalism is the unrolling of the modern, emancipatory compromise. It's precisely so freedom and equality can reign that laws have multiplied and become more precise, more insensitive, more bewildering.

'All of these ideas are a part of your lives and nowadays none of you would know how to live without them. But imagine the upset they must have caused when they were introduced. The first Carlists spoke and wrote in a strange way. In all their declarations there isn't a single grievance or proposal or phrase that can be translated into today's language. There's merely a continuous emphasis upon certain magic words. "Long live Charles v and the Spanish Inquisition!" This absurd cry alone mobilised thousands of peasants and weavers. Naturally, there was an element of coercion – inseparable from any military confrontation – and some joined up because the Carlists were paying more than the Liberals. But it's impossible to stage a civil war of that size without believable language. And perhaps one of the biggest clashes was between the old way of speaking and the rhetoric of the civil servants, judges and diplomats spearheading the new modern State. The Carlists are a part of the prehistory you all carry within and you won't escape it so easily.'

That use of the second-person plural always got on my nerves. Years ago, R. would often use it in class, with a tone somewhere between admonition and irony. His classes were from a time when educational psychology had yet to become the academic-bureaucratic business it is today. Or perhaps not. There may well have already been educational psychologists professionally dedicated to destroying any possibility of an intelligent teacher-student relationship. But R. had not got the memo. Despite only being two generations older than me, it felt as though four or five separated us and he had always seemed immune to institutional idiocies. He had absorbed his education sensuously with the same seriousness given to his sensory knowledge of wine, gastronomy, and good conversation. That was why in class he was capable of becoming infuriated with an idea or an author with the same swiftness and unpredictability that he might become captivated by an atmosphere, the look of a stranger or the taste of a tomato well nourished by sun and soil. More than the actual content of his classes, it's the anarchic passion with which he taught that I remember most. In fact, the real lesson that he taught us was, ultimately, that anarchic passion itself.

'Now, I'd like you to consider this,' he continued. 'Wielemann and Foraster are educated men surrounded by people who are barely even literate. Their heads are jam-packed with learned concepts and thoughts, and now and again they get carried away with the extravagant combinations they create. Perhaps there's no other environment that could have tickled their fancy quite like that one did. One took pleasure in his confusion, the other suffered and fell ill. Perhaps neither would have been able to say just what they were learning there. Perhaps it was the best thing that could have happened to them.'

We turned onto a tarmacked road without a single car in sight, arriving a few minutes later at the farmhouse where my paternal ancestors had lived. When we had visited it with my grandfather twenty years ago, it had been a deserted ruin lost in a landscape that no longer had any need for men. Now, newly restored, it was surrounded by immaculately arranged flower beds and had three shiny cars parked on the threshing floor. As we neared the house, I realised that on the other side of the road an elderly man was watering a plant. He was stark naked. His stomach skin drooped down giving him two marsupial pouches, held in place by a narrow backside and two chicken legs. A dazzling white blob under the sun. When he saw us, he slowly crossed the road, hid himself behind a pillar at the front of the house and then poked his smiling face out to ask if we were lost. R. wished him a pleasant morning with that deep voice of his.

The road continued to weave up ahead. Though sweating like pigs, it had not occurred to either of us to stop. R. pointed towards the woods and mountains, excitedly raising the volume of his voice on occasion. We found ourselves standing in front of Saint Martin's Church. I went into the overgrown graveyard where there were only two crosses with flowers in a clearing. The old vaults next to them merely served to hold up the slope. We approached the ancient tower that had witnessed everything we had been discussing during our walk, resisting the weight of the centuries as best it could. All around it were fallen stones and castle ruins. Withered vines clung to the walls and further up, as if horrified to find themselves there, the skeletal trees eked out a miserable existence. Walking back, I allowed my gaze to wander slowly over the valley before R.'s shout startled me.

'It's already after one! How on earth are we going to get back?'

I thought about the Lichnowsky chapter on my desk, more than six miles from those woods.

'Hang on.'

He proceeded to pull out a mobile phone the size of a shoe and dialled a number.

'Listen, er, I bumped into Raül... yes, we've been walking. Look, we lost track of time and we've ended up in Riner...No, no, we lost track of time, that's all, you know how it is, once we get talking... Along the river... Well, we didn't realise, you see. And now it's late, it's almost lunchtime, and it's hot enough to scald a lizard out here. It's been a beautiful day, we've seen loads of blue tits... Sorry, you're right, I'm twittering on... Yes, lunch, of course, I'm sorry... Are you sure you don't mind? Raül, she's coming to pick us up. Darling, we really appreciate it. It'd be a bit tricky getting back on foot. God, it's hot... Yes, sorry, you know how it is... Duck breast? I say! Raül, I'm being wined and dined! We'll be waiting for you at Riner Castle. Thank you so much, I really don't know what I'd do without you... OK, I'm twittering on, sorry.'

Twenty minutes later, Joana found us sitting shirtless on the grass, both gleaming with sweat, a round torso next to a scrawny one, our faces the colour of burning embers and our eyes full of embarrassment.

9

Wars, like narratives, have a culminating point of maximum symbolic plasticity, though rarely does this moment of climax coincide with that of the stories we tell about them. In September 1837, accompanied by Prince von Lichnowsky and his fellow Prussians, and trailing an army of priests, noblemen, bureaucrats, and the thousands of marching feet belonging to his volunteers, Charles Maria Isidre de Borbó bore down on Madrid, a city which, owing its entire existence to politics, holds a permanent and pathological fascination over the politically minded. The monarch dominated by symbols – who had been placed at the forefront of a war over the control of symbols, who allowed himself to be seduced and amused by the sound of words but then appalled to find himself faced with bleak reality and who, despite his constant claims, still wasn't king but nothing more than an enthusiastic proclamation repeated in hundreds of inhospitable locations – found himself before the symbolic city par excellence. Now was the moment to make the definitive step, to join these two symbols together and set the world spinning on its axis. While governmental Spain was filled with antipathy, contempt and conceit, a wave of fervour was flooding Carlist Spain.

Yet, at the gates to Madrid, Charles Maria Isidre de Borbó began to have doubts. The usurping government had sent ambiguous messages. The destructive fire of revolution had spread and the nobility's age-old privileges supressed, but recently a backwards step had been taken, quite possibly in the spirit of conciliation. Nevertheless, the meandering indecision of the Liberals disorientated him, for he was a man who much preferred being carried away by metaphysical rallying calls and overawed by evocations than being forced to face facts. But this time things were different: Don Charles, the symbol in body form, now stood before Madrid, the symbol in city form, watched the ancient aureoles evaporate and it dawned on him that his unconditional love for the city's inhabitants was, in all likelihood, not reciprocated with the same unconditional and unshakeable faith. He realised he would have to get them onside with some slightly forced violence, lacking the religious fanaticism that gives meaning to any extermination. Quite possibly for the first time in his entire life, the consequences of the decisions he was about to make presented themselves with the utmost clarity before his watery and asymmetric eyes in advance. He tried to bring order to his features but they resisted his authority and he began to teeter, just as he had during his truly triumphant entrance a few weeks earlier in the midst of those enraptured, roaring, crazed crowds, only this time there was no tall red-headed Prussian poised and ready to rescue him and the king tumbled to the ground, alone, consternation clinging to his eyes, his crooked moustache and his partially open mouth. Straightening his tunic, he ordered an immediate retreat without admitting a single word of dissent. The feet of his volunteers followed him with a faith that remained stuck to the walls of that city turned symbol before melting, trickling down and finally evaporating as though it had never existed. The enraged protest of a handful of officers found nothing solid to bounce off and there is surely nothing more difficult than directing your anger at a desolate void.

In Solsona, while news of this denouement had yet to arrive, the fervour was made of a tense, durable, yet slightly elastic material composed in equal parts of concern and expectation and the men's conversations were little more than an excited flurry of exclamations, interrogations and loosely connected names. It was as if nothing definite needed to be discussed in order to speak about that other thing, yet speaking about that other thing meant not talking about anything definite, instead filling the wait with vacuities. The few times Wielemann left the confines of the house he immediately grasped the meaning of those conversations for they chimed perfectly with the state of apathy and inarticulate lassitude into which he had been plunged over the course of the previous few days. Wielemann was still young enough to believe that sadness was equivalent to lamenting, shedding tears, banging one's head against the wall and other such exaggerated forms of being out of one's mind, hence why he failed to comprehend the icy and inexpressive intensity that had left him so despondent. He peered inside himself and saw nothing but emptiness and therefore believed he was free of anguish. But when Wielemann got wind of the royal retreat he felt a painful stabbing in his stomach and, just like a house that has long ago crumbled on the inside while preserving its façade tumbles with the gentlest of blows to reveal all which never existed, he no longer pondered the point of his adventure, nor the possibility of coming out of it unscathed, but instead sank deeper into his own bitter dejection. Fortunately for him, the stabbing in his stomach intensified and the pain overpowered his apathy. Eventually, he went to see Foraster with the aim of hiding the fact that what he really needed was a doctor.

He passed the same enormous, ever-present pot boiling over the fire and the wide, weary-looking old woman tending to it, the two of them submerged in a thick, foggy fragrance as indistinct as it was indifferent. Foraster invited him to play the piano. Wielemann ran his fingers reluctantly over the keys and could manage only a few inexpressive scales and aimless harmonies, fruitlessly attempting the opening of three or four early compositions before trying a melody from the last movement of Beethoven's first sonata which usually made him quiver with joy. After just a few bars he came to a grinding halt, prompting Foraster to stare at him with an intense, inquiring look. Wielemann collapsed into the armchair while sighing heavily, every line on his face confessing his dejection, before finally mustering the strength to utter something in his heavily accented French:

'What do you do here exactly?'

More than a question formulated out of interest, it was a cry for help. Foraster experienced one of those convulsions which, despite not being externally visible, feel like a snake slipping through your insides before disappearing, its only external effect being to make one even more motionless and marble-like and to insinuate that any reaction is on par with the irretrievable heroism of antiquity. Wielemann uttered another cry:

'I came to fight on behalf of Order and the King.'

The same snake slipped through Foraster again but this time it served to bring him to his senses.

'Here they use similar words, but they move them around a bit. Here it's: for King and Catholicism.'

'Well, I wanted to restore order. I mean, alongside those who also want to restore it. But I can't make sense of anything. They won't give me any commands.'

'Ah, well, there's nothing strange about that. I said that here they fight in the name of King and Catholicism. I didn't say anything about order. You see, the King and God have a distinct advantage: they remain far, far away in the distance, even when they're right in front of your nose. The more power they have, the less we have to worry ourselves with order. They're handy, don't you see? There's nothing like a few solemn images to clear your head and cleanse yourself of all the muck. Order's an albatross.'

Wielemann looked at him with a blank stare that Foraster took as an invitation to continue.

'My job is to stem the flow of bleeding and charlatans. That's what I do here. This month alone I've successfully amputated the limbs of twenty soldiers. I'm a representative of medical science in this quagmire full of earthworms and murky passions. No, not a representative: a loyal servant of science. While they all race towards an early grave, I contemplate, apply my learning, and save whoever I can. Like an explorer, I wade through the darkness with my luggage: surgical precision, chemical reactions, and vaccines.

Where the chaos of man reigns, I do my utmost to master nature, to harness its laws and curtail disaster. Because there's an order that doesn't hang heavy around one's neck: it's the order above us, under us and inside us all, the same predestined order we've been scrutinising and slowly decoding for thousands of years and which one day we might even fully comprehend. That day science and the world will be two separate words meaning the same thing. No longer will we be able to say that man is a slave to nature, or that he dominates it. Man will possess science and science will possess man. Man will do what he wants and want what he does because the profound order of the world will coincide with his ideas and aspirations. Man will finally be the centre and the pinnacle of Creation. And that's how I go about lopping limbs off Carlists. They're a small obstacle on the path to knowledge, a carbuncle of stubborn ignorance, but I suppose they must exist for some reason or other. In any case, with their arms and legs chopped off they take up less space and the city can breathe more easily.'

Wielemann's face turned rigid and he sat up stiffly in the armchair. A stabbing pain shot through him from his left shoulder down to his right kidney. Foraster instinctively adopted a professional demeanour and took his pulse while asking if he felt dizzy. Not even in his native German could Wielemann find the words to explain what was happening to him and as he prepared himself to merely confess his despair, his mouth became filled with a dense saliva he was capable of swallowing only by chewing. He remained quiet for much longer than usual, using the silence as armour against the undefined. Foraster observed the deathly pallor of his skin without daring to say a word and started to walk up and down the room. Prompted either by the sound of the doctor's pacing or the consternation it communicated, a soft but assured voice was finally heard, detached but displaying a slightly condescending tone on the final syllables, as though uttered with the infinite patience required to endure the ignorance of learned men:

'He's all out of sorts, cock.'

Foraster spun around in the direction of the old woman and was liberated from doubt. Wrapping an arm around Wielemann's back, he slowly helped him to his feet. They passed the kitchen where the old woman and the even older pot were still sitting, absent and inert, as though having had nothing to do with events, and went down into the street. A few minutes later, they entered a tall, narrow house and found themselves inside a room with a dozen chairs occupied by people of all ages and manner of clothing. Instead of sitting, they appeared to be pasted to the chairs, their emaciated bodies retaining just the necessary life force to stave off the decomposition process. Those slumping, sleepy masses of flesh shared the same slow, measured breathing, with the slight hint of a snore, and it didn't take long for Wiele-mann to involuntarily join their catatonic symphony, inhaling and exhaling with his eyes half closed and his mouth ajar. Apart from Foraster, who stood guard by Wielemann's side, the only thing amid those four walls was the swell of their pain-ridden, almost vegetative, slumber, each of them wrapped in their own heavy, private darkness. The entire notion of time had disa-ppeared, leaving only a static transience which came from and went nowhere and for that reason was all the more noticeable when the door suddenly sprang open and a young man gathered up, like someone grabbing hold of a parcel, the person sitting nearest. With the chair now vacant, each mass of flesh jumped in unison with a dank, muffled sound onto the seat to their left and the sluggish swell rose up again at once, caressing each of them like a soft fur. Wielemann allowed the current to carry him away while Foraster kicked hard against it.

After much opening and slamming of the door, it was finally Wielemann's turn to be seized by the young man. He was helped up a steep flight of stairs that seemed to narrow until disappea-ring into the darkness. At the top, another door opened and they found themselves in a room that looked exactly the same as the previous one and was also heaving with pulpy masses united by a common somnolence. Wielemann abandoned himself to it once more whereas Foraster did his best to stay on his toes.

After more comings and goings and yet more shuffling between seats, they were dragged up another flight of stairs, only this time much darker and narrower, and left in an identical room – the same one, for all they knew – with the same masses composed of little more than flesh and breathing.

Finally, they scrambled up an almost vertical flight shrouded in absolute darkness. Wielemann advanced on autopilot but Foraster was nearing the end of his tether. This time the door opened to reveal a brightly lit room with a large window looking out onto the mountains of the Port del Comte, so dark and imposing that they appeared much closer than they actually were. Sitting waiting for them in a low armchair was a man of about fifty with long, spindly legs whose knees reached almost all the way up to his mouth, making him look like an expectant grasshopper. His bulging eyes seemed superimposed onto his face, as if taken from another body or another world, and were joined to his taut lips by a perfectly straight nose. His voice was deep, authoritative and slightly hoarse, but welcoming nonetheless.

'And what brings you to this neck of the woods?'

'This gentleman…'

'Out of sorts?'

'So Nana says.'

Without the least sign of effort, the man got up to the most incredible height – he was almost twice the size of Foraster and a good few inches taller than Wielemann – and stood framed by the window with the fields at his knees, the mountains by his waist, and the clouds circling his head, his figure converted into a pillar of darkness amid the resplendence of nature. Taking a long object out of the cabinet, he went up to the still-sleepy Wielemann and raised what could now be seen to be a hammer high above his head in order to bring it down with maximum force. Despite his drowsiness, Wielemann started to open his mouth and eyes, more in disbelief than panic. The man laughed mockingly and tossed the instrument to one side.

'Joan, please,' protested Foraster while exhaling through his nose with indignation.

'Alright, alright. But where on earth did you find this man?'

While referring to him he gently stroked his head as if he were a small child but Wielemann, who was starting to come round, shrunk back in bewilderment. The man then took a medallion displaying the image of Our Lady of the Cloister out of his pocket and held the chain aloft between thumb and forefinger. Keeping it perfectly still, he stared at the foreigner with a calmness immersed in itself almost to the point of absence and nourished by the certainty of the centuries. He then muttered something long and difficult to understand, perhaps even unintelligible. With a gesture that could well have been caused by a sense of shame but was most likely out of fear and reverence for the all too familiar, Foraster looked away. It was over in a few seconds. That unspeakably tall man turned and went over to the window whereupon he assumed a dark, motionless, and somewhat cumbersome shape like a sculpture carved clumsily out of charcoal.

'All done.'

'Thanks, Joan. I'll save you some chard and aubergines.'

This time the man didn't turn around. A sound similar to an acknowledgement, which didn't seem to have been uttered by any mouth but instead having emanated from that static figure, crept cautiously across the room and came to rest upon the visitors before slipping slowly down them like a loving embrace. Wielemann was sure they had left the room by the same door they had used to enter it but this time the stairs were not only wider and brighter but also seemed shorter and not nearly as precipitous. Once again, Foraster wrapped his arm around his back but Wielemann no longer needed any help. As he strode with newfound strength, he looked over at his companion in complete confusion. Lying in bed that evening he noticed not only how the sheets caressed him but how the weight of his body enabled him to rest more peacefully and without any of those agonising thoughts. He began to write in his diary that he had gone to see a witchdoctor, a healer 'as they say here', but he felt far too healthy and happy to be hunched over the page like that. He fell asleep without a worry in the world. Not a single noise disturbed the night.

'Mushrooms!'

It was the first time Foraster had presented himself at the widow's house. He was standing at the front door rocking nervously from one leg to the other with an over-the-top, barely containable and somewhat childish smile stretched across his face. He then set off down the street, almost dragging Wielemann by the sleeve.

They entered his house, passed the pot and the old woman and went to sit down in the living room in the fading glow of the setting sun.

'Are you feeling any better?'

The wind began to howl, darkness filled the room and a burst of raindrops appeared on the glass planes of the crooked windows. Foraster set about arranging the firewood with an iron, positioning the knobbly branches at the bottom and the thick log on top. He then filled the gaps with wood shavings and lit them with the candle.

'Oh yes, much better, thank you.'

A flame spread as though it were a single breath before settling down modestly and patiently. Wielemann could already note the drop in temperature and he edged his armchair forwards in search of the fire's warmth as the flame from the burning branches began to wrap itself around the log.

'So, are you a bona fide Carlist, then?'

Wielemann, transfixed by the fire's undulating yellows, had

become so immersed in the moment that he made no attempt to comprehend what had just been said. The flames performed a serene, delicate dance devoid of repetitions or surprises and projected gigantic shadows upon the walls. Dark, wordless ideas sparked and crackled inside his head.

Without realising he had even left the room, Wielemann looked up to see the doctor returning from the kitchen with two glasses of red wine.

'I doubt very much that Beethoven of yours was…'

All at once, Wielemann came to his senses and tried to work out where that comment had come from. 'That Beethoven of yours' had been uttered with the playful provocation of a friend but Wielemann still preferred to seek shelter in the safety of banal conversation.

'Do you live alone?'

'With Nana.'

With an apologetic look, he tried a different approach.

'Is the rest of the family off fighting?'

'Good heavens, no. The war came much too late for them. My mother died when I was born. My father died of an injury he sustained to the thigh fighting that Frenchman's war. It was a slow, intimate wound that kept him company for five years. It would scar over and then open up like a poisonous flower, closing again only to split open once more. He had plenty of time to chew things over, as Grandpa always used to say. Can you imagine? All day glued to the armchair you're sat in now. He'd just sit staring at and stroking it like it was some defenceless animal. He'd talk to it, poke fun at it under his breath, even tell it stories about my mother. Tears would run down his face when he saw the wound start to weep, and the two of them would secrete their deepest fears together. Anyway, in the end it turned gangrenous and they had to amputate his leg. I don't know what he was more upset about: losing his leg or losing the wound. But soon they realised they hadn't cut high enough and that's when he really began to think, only now not a single word crossed his lips. The fellow had never had any expensive habits or vices and, well, that was now completely out of the question even if he'd wanted one. He got the idea of sending me to the Royal School of Medicine and Surgery, so he took all the money he'd earned at the glass factory and put it in the hands of some broker so it would grow. Oh, and it grew alright. After some more time spent thinking, he died, and I was probably the first member of the family to ever live in Barcelona. With the leftover money I bought a few books and my Otter & Kyburz.'

He turned to prod the embers. More than the story, what surprised Wielemann was the manner in which he spoke about his father, without the merest hint of bitterness, complaint, or doubt, as though he were describing some inevitable natural phenomenon. He thought about his own father, dictating a letter with martial rhythm while quick marching from one side of the library to the other; his mother, who always had the perfect phrase for any social occasion; his sister in Paris, married to the Ambassador to France; his brother, busy working his way up the military hierarchy; and his uncle, sat among the general staff of the Kingdom of Prussia. It warmed his heart to picture his family safe, healthy and, most importantly, alive. In that perfectly oiled machine, he was the only faulty cog. A spark followed by a bursting flame snapped him out of his reverie.

'But you returned to Solsona,' stated Wielemann, careful to conceal his amazement.

'There was Grandpa...Nana...'

'You want your soup now, cock?'

Foraster went into the kitchen and emerged with a tray of mushrooms and sausages. Spreading the embers with the iron, he placed the grill on top of them and proceeded to lay the mushrooms out with a mixture of reverential finesse and stifled rapacity. As he sprinkled them with olive oil and salt, the room began to fill with the fragrance of the forest floor.

The meat was then carefully placed around the edge of the grill and they went to sit at table. The old woman brought them two earthenware bowls brimming with piping hot onion soup full of mysterious material floating in it like half-disintegrated ruins. It had a carefully crafted, intense, and slightly bitter taste. In his attempt to decipher the swirling composition of that patiently made meal, Wielemann had the impression of entering a dark world of primeval matter ordered by Time's inaccessible reason. The old woman sat down at the end of the table with her bowl and peered in silence at the men, from the darkness, guarded by the deformed figures of the shadows dancing on the wall.

'Is there really as much turmoil in Barcelona as they say?'

'Well, it's certainly a good place for theorising, that I can tell you. There are plenty of down-and-outs starving to death, bourgeois riding up and down in expensive carriages and bureaucrats speaking in that sort of solid but haughty Castilian forged over centuries in the palaces of Madrid. All in all, it makes a certain impression, and it does wonders for the imagination. You take a few good-for-nothings, stick them behind a barricade and immediately you're inundated by a swarm of scholars, the sort that solve all of humanity's ills with a newspaper article. Catholicism is even more deeply rooted there than it is here and they lean heavily towards symbolism. And when they're riled, boy, do they burn monasteries with passion. But they also have their shortcomings. On every corner there's someone who's discovered one of the many truths for sale at a cut price. It's a never-ending parade of pathetic deposed gods, addicted to drama, who'd devour their own sons for a scrap of attention. Despite having my fair share of fun, it started to wear thin, until one summer I decided to return to Solsona and, well, it revitalised me to a degree. When the guerrillas started running amok in the woods and setting fire to town halls, I figured from here I'd have an interesting angle to contemplate the gradual destruction of everything. That and the fireplace, of course.'

Foraster went to inspect the mushrooms sweating over the embers and carefully turned them one by one.

'In Barcelona I made the acquaintance of a gentleman from Strasbourg. More German than French. He was strange: a Protestant. Are you Protestant as well?'

'I'm religious. I don't know if I'm merely Protestant.'

The doctor peered at him from the shadows with his head leant back and his eyes narrowed as though a great distance had been placed between them.

'What I mean is I have a strong religious sentiment.'

The doctor opened his eyes wide and cocked his head to one side with an expression of both curiosity and suspicion.

'What I really mean is… You know how when we look at the outline of the city and we see the houses reaching upwards, piled one on top of the other, all trying to climb higher even though they can't, but we never doubt for a moment where they are pointing? Or when we marvel at some huge mountain, but God isn't in the mountain, therefore while we're looking at it we contemplate God with eyes that aren't our own? It's the Infinite that appears in finite things, the Absolute that we equally see and don't see in nature, the Eternal that we perceive but which slips away from us with each passing moment. It's an intuition without history, credo, or words. Knowing we depend wholly on something we can never actually know, a hallowed void we'll never be capable of completely filling: that is faith. Afterwards come pomp, convention, adornment, and images. Things that, frankly speaking, leave me cold. Trying to snare God is the surest way of expelling Him. I believe in Christ because he's a God that brings the divine down to the level of flesh, blood and nail clippings, to corruptible material. The cross is the instrument that nails our dreams to the solid ground, placating them yet, at the same time, always pointing upwards…'

Surprised by the emotion that had gripped his guest, Foraster nodded in agreement, more on account of the eloquence of the discourse than the thinking behind it. The crackle of two sparks in quick succession reminded him of the mushrooms. Grabbing hold of the grill, he shook it gently under his nose and closed his eyes as he inhaled deeply. The old woman returned with three plates, licking her lips.

Encircled by the dancing shadows, Wielemann stared intently at those spongy, oily shapes wrapped in a delicate layer of vibrant light the colour of an autumnal forest. Emanating from them was the remote life of places forgotten and unfrequented by man, which are almost all the places in the world, full of tense and ephemeral crescendos, reiterated with the self-assuredness of things that have yet to experience betrayal or despair. Under his fork, the spongy shapes gave way passively but, once inside his mouth, they exploded with all the aromas and tastes of the undergrowth, of worms and wild boars, ferrets and excrement, seeds, snails, and decomposing leaves. Wielemann lost himself in plant and animal memory, in the memory of all those who had lost themselves in it before him. Foraster smiled.

'We Catholics have the distinct advantage of not having to believe in anything. All we need is a cathedral, a handful of saints and a couple of cassocks to maintain convention. Take me, for example. I'm an atheist but no one can deny my deep Catholicism. The Holy Inquisition that your lot defend would tremble to see the importance Protestants put on mystic experiences, faith, Christ, and a whole host of other insignificant things. Barbarians! We Catholics, thank our lucky stars, haven't seen or heard Jesus in almost two thousand years. In that respect, atheists and believers – to put it in those terms – are exactly the same. And long may it continue that way.'

'Cynicism…' blurted Wielemann. He had intended only to make the conventional display of displeasure that protocol demanded of him but halfway through he had sensed the intonation wasn't quite right and had tried to turn it into a question but, discovering it was too late, had left the word hanging there between two contradictory intentions.

'Not at all. Or do you believe life is made up of such outlandish things as... um... er... faith as a tangible experience? Hogwash. That's been around for five minutes and was no doubt a northern invention... like the vaccine. People are more resistant than philosophical treatises give them credit for; they're made of routine habits and empty words. An external and entirely visible structure holds us in place. Why, saints carved out of wood have done more in this world than any real-life saint ever has. And tell me, why shouldn't we find that marvellous? Why do we have to believe that behind every word, in every honest person, there must be an intimate, integral and authentic vibration perfectly in tune with the vowels and consonants of some intelligible language?'

'But the other day... about vaccines... you said...'

'Well, that depends, like everything in life... Just look at this beautiful mushroom! Ain't that something, huh?' Foraster raised it aloft ceremoniously, exhibiting an intense, shiny, oily object with scarlet and ochre tones. It was the first time he had spoken to Wielemann like that, so informally. He chewed slowly and rolled his eyes with glee before continuing as if having suddenly remembered a sentence that had been left unfinished.

'Anyway... what you say about religion... how does that tie in with the proclamations your Carlists like to make? Have you worked out why you came to fight this war yet?' Foraster had stressed the word *your* with provocative irony in the hope something might come of it.

Wielemann bit blissfully into a mushroom. It was like eating a kind of weightless, porous material, a delicious vacuity that didn't sit on the stomach.

'If I've understood correctly, you speak of a chain of isolated individual revolutions that illuminate everything for an instant and are then extinguished again, free from dogmas and churches. Your Carlists, however, want the exact opposite: no one is to lay so much as a finger on the Church or its doctrines so that everyone can happily keep on playing the brute without worrying where the world is headed.'

A thought occurred to Wielemann.

'That reminds me of a story about a singer from Berlin. A truly splendid soprano with the voice of a nightingale. Despite her lack of faith, she was at her most impressive when singing sacred music. In the middle of all those pompous polyphonies laden with ceremony, her elegant voice went straight to the heart. Bettine... the soprano in question... was loved by everyone and could perform two or three concerts a day in different locations without showing the least sign of fatigue. She was like a fairy that flew from one place to another, made entirely of vibrating air and with only the illusion of a corporeal existence. It was thrilling to follow her and to note the different resonances her voice made in each temple. It was purely on account of her that I entered Saint Hedwig's Cathedral. It's a Catholic church, round and squat, and it can be rather suffocating, but when she sang there the walls became thinner and the dome slighter, as if a hand were raising it aloft. One Easter Sunday, she was there to perform the solos of one of those Italian masses stuffed with stodgy harmonies that always seem to arouse the weak at heart. But her ethereal intonations meant the music not only captivated me but also left me stunned. It was as if the cathedral were alive with a swarm of tiny angels as the sound of her voice skipped along those sluggish chords. And all the while, her gloriously godless humour tore through that patchwork of overly sentimental war- bling. For some unfathomable reason, it was precisely Bettine's light-heartedness that made the piece all the more solemn and beguiling. By the time we reached the Sanctus I was shaking from head to foot. *Sanctus, sanctus, sanctus.* A thick cloud of incense wafted through the cathedral. *Dominus Deus Sabaoth, pleni sunt cœli et terra gloria tua.* That was when I realised Bettine had edged towards the soprano section of the choir. After sharing a few clandestine exchanges with a tenor, she disappeared stage left. I felt abandoned. Now the music was like an empty shell. The walls closed in and the dome descended slowly and agonisingly. I left before mass ended and went running to another church where I knew Bettine was due to sing. But she wasn't there! Another soprano – competent at best – had stepped in for her. That afternoon I returned home sneezing so hard it made the walls shake. Just a few hours later I was confined to my bed with a fever. I wouldn't even know how to begin describing the images that appeared to me during my illness. When I began to feel better, I was informed Bettine had lost her voice immediately after performing at Saint Hedwig's.'

At the end of the table, the toothless old woman sat muttering that mysterious saint's name – 'edwig… 'edwig… Saint 'edwig… – while Foraster listened surrounded by shape-shifting shadows and, behind him, a slowly dying flame. He leant over to take the sausages off the grill and placed another log on the fire.

'She lost it right after speaking to that tenor. She told him she was in a hurry because not only was she due to perform a cantata at another church, but she had yet to rehearse the duet she'd be singing at the home of some aristocrats later that evening. As she was saying that, the Sanctus rang out amid a cloud of incense. The tenor then whispered to her words that would haunt my fellow music lovers and me over the subsequent days: "Don't you know that leaving the temple during the *Sanctus* is an unpardonable sin? Why, soon you won't be able to sing in church, at all!" He was only joking, of course, but the words came out like a severe warning in a deep bass that didn't seem his own, making even him shudder. The moment she stepped foot outside she turned pale and lost her voice.'

Foraster's face lit up with a smile and he began to applaud.

'She lost her voice for weeks. The curse wasn't lifted until Bettine heard a group of people discussing her plight when they thought she was out of earshot. And without having understood a thing, she recovered her voice. The last time I saw her she was as playful and impious as ever. But now she always waits until the very last note of the *Sanctus* is played before leaving church.'

'You see, you see?' said the doctor with delight.

The two of them ate concealing their excitement and for a good while neither added a word to the unanimous feelings swirling around the room. Outside it was already dark and the rain had stopped but inside the fire was burning brightly. After swallowing the last remaining slice of sausage and taking another swig of wine, Wielemann went to sit down at the piano. He began a fantastical *andante* with a melody that unfolded cautiously, revealing itself momentarily and then retreating, all the while getting quicker and quicker yet never losing its poise, before bursting free for a few seconds with a series of frenetic arpeggios and ending with a steady calmness, smiling like the three people in the room. With only the merest of glances and without waiting, Wielemann launched into the rippling and melancholic joy of the second movement, now *staccato*, now *legato*, the measured harmonies of which seemed constantly on the verge of spilling over uncontrollably. The pianist felt the fire on his back like a warm caress. The stocky old woman remained at the end of the table with her hands in her lap while those restless, dancing notes filled the room, leapt out of the window, scattered along the rain-soaked street and sneaked into the houses under the cover of darkness. The neighbours stopped peeling potatoes, tucking children into bed, changing into nightclothes, making love, even praying, each one of them raising their head to hear that joyous melody from another world coming to greet them in the cold dark of night. It only lasted a moment. Soon the music – *adagio con espressione, allegro vivace, presto* – was lost among the walls, the shadows, the fresh air and the low, overcast sky. The neighbours could no longer hear it and they returned to their evening tasks. At Foraster's house the fire continued to burn long into the night.

10

I move words from one page to another. There's a moment when the translation advances by itself, as though the equivalences were automatic and I were a simple machine. For Lichnowsky and Wielemann, however, stranded in that strange world, theirs must have been an altogether different experience. Those place names, full of peculiar resonances, must have sounded more impenetrable than the rocks crashing down the mountainside or the howl of some forest beast. The bureaucratic efficiency they had been taught in Prussia collided head on with obstinate reality. Lichnowsky writes:

The only measure introduced by General Royo was a division into companies, meaning that each cohort and their commander received a number and was transformed into an official unit under the command of a captain. These captains referred to the men they had enlisted in their native valleys as 'their boys' and the troops were called this or that captain's 'boys', as if they were his personal lackeys. Furthermore, in Catalonia no guerrilla is known by his real name but instead by a *nom de guerre*, ensuring that no one outside of the province might decipher these designations. Porredon, Pons, Ibáñez, Sobrevias and Tristany signed their reports with their real names but their guerrillas were called 'Ros d'Eroles' boys', 'Pep de l'Oli's boys', 'Llarg de Copons' boys', 'Muchacho's boys' and 'Father Benet's boys', the result being that very few soldiers knew their captain's actual name and almost none of them knew that of those further up the command chain. This confusion made it nigh on impossible to punish the captains or to relieve them of their duties. The innocuous appearance of this deep-rooted tradition belied its many grave consequences.

It must have been incredibly frustrating from a Prussian's point of view. When referring to all this, another visitor from the north – Wilhelm von Rahden – could only call on the fanciful images he had garnered from exotic travel books. It was his only way of bridging the abyss that separated him and his compatriots from that dark savagery, a chasm as deep as time and space:

For the most part, Catalan troops still lived and fought in a half-primitive state. The horsemen looked like centaurs, given they went almost completely disrobed and the majority of them rode bareback. They were armed with spears and, on occasion, bows and arrows. Coloured blankets flapped around their waists. Infantry soldiers had only a few long-range rifles between them, some of which were still equipped with matchlocks, and the gleaming daggers hanging from their hips made them look like Bedouin. More often than not, they only had three or four cartridges, which they carried on their chest next to a devotional scapular. Food and other provisions were carried inside garishly coloured woollen blankets and on their heads they sported bright red hats ending in a point that fell down their backs.

11

'I can do it.'

'I'd understand if you didn't want to.'

'It's no bother.'

'I won't breathe a word of it to anyone. Don't worry.'

'It's all the same to me.'

'Honestly, no one will find out. I'd understand if your principles...'

'If you keep on like that then perhaps I really will change my mind.'

'I'd understand, I really would.'

'Alright, cut it out. Tell me what you want it to say.'

'OK... that I left home half a year ago...'

Foraster began to write while silently mouthing the words to himself: A considerable time ago, I departed disciplined Prussia, bastion of legitimist Europe...

'... because my father wanted to, er... make me worthy of the family name...'

... heeding the triumphant trumpet call of our rightful sovereign Augustus Don Charles v (may God protect him) and his crusaders and, in this manner, ensuring the continuance of a sacrosanct family tradition of loyalty to secular order.

'... but I lost my uncle's letter of recommendation...'

Notwithstanding, owing in all likelihood to the intervention of some malefic Liberal agent, I was divested of all documentation, including an affectionate missive from the pen of a highly-respected Prussian nobleman and, disorientated and dispossessed, I found myself alone in a dark wilderness replete with unfamiliar signs and impenetrable beings, my only consolation being my faith in the Lord and our illustrious legitimate Sovereign (may God protect him)...

'But I need a post, a mission and a way of returning home

once I've served the cause.'

... thus I find myself obliged to petition, with my most sincere humility and fanatical fervour for Legitimacy, that the authorities may deign to concede me a secondary position, yet one in accordance with my passion and breeding, if possible in this here city of Solsona, tenebrous and disconcerting for some, but known to many for its obstinate insistence upon preserving all that which may be considered worthy of preservation, a position that bestows upon my humble self the indubitable honour of serving the Restoration of Order, the Immobility of Time, and the Alleviation of all Roman Catholics. Long live the King and the Holy Spanish Inquisition (may God protect them).

Foraster handed the sheet of paper to Wielemann with a low, theatrical bow and the Prussian ran his eyes over the text, pausing sceptically after each sentence.

'Really? That's how you'd say it? Are you sure?'

'It's Carlist rhetoric,' said the doctor, lounging back in his armchair and looking at him with a tired smile.

Wielemann had left home that morning with the satisfaction of having finally decided upon a definite course of action. The lethargy of the previous weeks – as familiar to him now as a domesticated animal – was pleasing and painful for precisely the same reason: it didn't require him to do anything. The letter, if nothing else, might help to remedy any remaining regrets. He left the letter to cool for a few days before finally putting it in the inside pocket of his overcoat, just as he had done with the original one. While out walking, he had the habit of patting it to note the feeling of fulfilled duty without knowing who he had to hand it to or being overly concerned about finding out.

Winter was already fast approaching. To the north, the Port del Comte appeared behind a filthy white veil and on the outskirts of the city the little green that still held onto life, now fragile and almost grey, trembled as though intimidated by the air itself. The carts creaked miserably behind the sleepy and stubborn donkeys. All along the streets, people walked hunched up to protect themselves from the elements.

The widow went about her household chores wrapped in a long, thick blanket made of black wool, the polar opposite of her white hair, often stopping to rub her hands together in front of the fire. From his seat by the window, Wielemann gazed at her with interest. Sleeping just a few metres from one another, they crossed paths numerous times a day but they never said a word to each other barring some commonplace courtesy which only served to make the silence even more impenetrable. To the foreign lodger, she was nothing more than a sequence of movements, a series of endless, transparent and, for that reason, utterly incomprehensible routines. When the widow moved away from the fire, he would add more wood and fan the flames so she might find the room warmer upon her return. Afterwards, he would go back to silently observing her. And so the days and nights passed.

It was the fifteenth of November and five months had gone by since the solitary Prussian first stepped foot in Solsona. He couldn't believe how the months had managed to pass so quickly, so aimlessly. When he looked back over it all, not a single significant event sprung to mind, merely a feeling of vagueness and, more recently, of a warm and hitherto unknown humanity. He had the premonition that he would end up trapped there for decades.

One afternoon, he was walking up Castell Street with his hand wedged in the inside pocket of his overcoat. Did he really have to do anything? He ruled out heroisms and humiliations: his father didn't deserve it, in either sense of the word. The street snaked upwards to the Hores bell tower where it flattened before straightening out to reveal a procession of modest houses preserved by a past resilience that inspired respect for things built to last. Wielemann found himself in front of the city hall. One of the two doors was open and there was no one to be seen inside. He could walk in, try giving the letter to someone, fail and go home with his conscience clear.

The foyer was gripped by a dark, eerie silence and Wielemann looked around for something that might help him orientate himself before trying his luck with the stairs. The walls were tall, bare, and unforgiving. To the right, behind an empty table, he saw a broad shadow. As he walked up to it, it seemed devoid of life but he slowly began to make out a humanoid shape: a bald, miniscule head was resting upon an enormous spherical torso like a globe from which emerged four tiny limbs. Sitting in a chair with a brazier underneath it for warmth, this life form had its eyes closed and the thinnest of gaps between its purple lips, not making the slightest movement. Wielemann leant on the table and slid slowly over to him. Within that vegetative stillness was some sort of minimal breathing, as though taking place deep down inside a disproportionately small lung wrapped in layers and layers of protective fat. Wielemann reached a hand forwards to touch what in any other person would have been their back, but at the last moment he lost his nerve. It scared, saddened, and distressed him to disrupt the concierge of sorts charged with guarding the entrance to a city hall during wartime and, anyway, it was starting to get chilly. He had done his duty and could now leave. But just as he was about to do exactly that, he felt a sneeze begin to rise up in him. It came from afar, giving him enough time to imagine the concierge sitting up with a start and interrogating him at the top of his voice before bundling him inside so the authorities could determine his intentions. With his eyes turning red, Wielemann resigned himself to his fate, raised his chin and let loose. The sheer force of the sneeze shook him from head to foot. Silence fell over the foyer again like a dark frozen mass. A few seconds went by in a state of paralysis before Wielemann started to creep away. At that point, the concierge's head detached itself slightly from the huge hunk of flesh and, opening its eyes ever so slightly, uttered a vague vowel somewhere between an 'i' and an 'e' with an inquiring air about it, before immediately retreating into the safety of its hermetic, indifferent, mollusc-like rotundity.

Now Wielemann was definitely on his way. But just as he was taking his first steps towards the exit, he heard someone coming down the stairs. He was surprised to see it was Foraster. The smiling doctor came striding towards him with a leather pouch – presumably full of coins – in his hand.

'I chop them into pieces and they keep on paying me!' he said into Wielemann's ear as loud as it was possible to say something without it going beyond the confines of a whisper.

Behind him, Josep Soler appeared like a shot, pushed the doctor aside and positioned himself close to Wielemann, as though wanting to protect him from some potent threat.

'Foreign sir! What a most welcome surprise!'

This was it. The moment for courage had arrived.

Je voudrais faire livraison d'une lettre à Monsieur le Maire ou à l'autorité militaire.

'*Ne vous inquietez pas.* I can take care of that for you,' replied Soler, edging forwards to within a hair's breadth of Wielemann's face. 'I can get all manner of messages to the military authorities, even to His Majesty, who still looks fondly on the hospitality he received from me one time. I'm an authority too, you know. Go on: I'm all ears.'

Wielemann looked around in search of help as Foraster waved goodbye to him from the doorway with the look of someone supressing a sadistic smile. The concierge remained immersed in his isolated mineral existence. Wielemann took the letter out of his inside pocket with the gesture of someone fulfilling an onerous obligation and placed it in his interlocutor's outstretched hand. Strenuous and baffled at first, Soler's expression gradually went from affectionate to incandescent to exultant. After each sentence, he looked up at the foreigner and offered him an operatic 'oh!' Upon finishing the letter he broke into a long silent applause – presumably out of respect for the concierge – and stared at him with a bucktoothed grin. He was welling up with tears such was his agitation.

'*Señor! Oh, señor!* I do prostrate at your feet with the most devout humility... prostrate?... prostate?... *Señor*, you have me at your illustrious feet with the most devout humility... my humility, not yours... you understand, right? *Quel admirable écrit, monsieur!* What a display of Carlist sincerity! You know something? The war would be over today if everyone was... er... were as steadfast as yourself, if everyone was... were... deep down, in their heart of hearts, as self-sacrificing. Oh, I thank the Lord for putting an ace like you up our sleeve! Providence, oh how I can feel Providence! How ungrateful and undeserving are the unbelievers of this world!' His face glowing red, Soler grabbed Wielemann by the hand. '*Señor!* I do solemnly swear to do everything in my power to make sure your letter is seen by the most honourable and sincere authorities, in accordance with your heartfelt conviction. I, in my capacity as a polyglot and a link in the chain of command, have access to the highest legitimist dignitaries in our kingdom. No doubt they'll communicate their response to me as a matter of urgency. If necessary, we'll go all the way to the top – to King Don Charles himself! We shalln't fail, sir. You're a top-notch Carlist, even if you ain't from round here. Put your faith in me. You'll be hearing from me soon enough. *Adiós, señor, adiós.* Blimey, with the Russians on our side we're sure to win! God certainly moves in mysterious ways!'

Those last words he uttered to himself as he began climbing the stairs, desperately racking his brains for a solution to such an important request. Wielemann, on the other hand, exited the building as fast as his legs would carry him. The sky was still clear, but a thick shadow had begun to engulf the street, gradually emptying it of people. The door suddenly slammed shut behind Wielemann with a heavy thud. Had the concierge unexpectedly come to life? Had a draught sealed the building?

Or had Soler merely been putting on a show and was in fact delighted to see the back of that foreign caller? Had he spoken to someone about that scene, Wielemann would no doubt have seen the funny side, but now he felt annoyed and a tad offended without knowing if it was on account of himself or the world, like someone who has just stubbed their toe twice in quick succession on the same table leg.

That night the black woollen blanket was nowhere near enough. Wielemann curled up and clutched it with all his might, as if the mere fact he was holding it tightly increased its capacity to keep him warm. In the depths of his sleep, the blanket became thicker and softer, acquiring a solid mammalian form that responded to his every move, first resembling a sheep, then a giant dog or bear, then a lioness with threatening claws that moved unpredictably, and finally a woman with brown sagging skin as soft as velvet yet, most importantly of all, warm, who hugged and kissed and licked him with a primitive passion that took even her by surprise. He was equally as surprised with himself as he ran his hands over her curves and penetrated her. He then felt something inexplicable: a warm and gooey substance was dribbling down his cheeks. He opened his eyes and saw, towering over him, the outline of a face with deformed features and absent-looking eyes, emitting a hot and heavy breath through its gaping mouth. As Wielemann cried out, the creature went running towards the door while producing something between a scream and a laugh. Wielemann remained frozen in bed, desperately trying to attach some human explanation to the shriek still echoing in his ears. When his body finally became responsive, he got out of bed and ran towards the door. Not a sound came from the living room or the kitchen. Putting his ear to the door of the widow's room, he heard a deep and rhythmic breathing. He looked over at the stairs and then up to a place he had never dared venture before. After climbing the first three steps, he stopped: he was sure he had heard a howl but there was nothing, just the same pure, everlasting silence. Had it all been just a dream? He went back down the stairs and looked over to the window. It was a clear night; too clear, perhaps. Everything had been left exposed as though privacy had been abolished. These are the moments when solitude seems the permanent state of things. Wielemann shivered, reached a hand up to his cheek, and felt the dark saliva. Back inside his room, he wedged a chair firmly against the door. Now the blanket was like a dead weight offering him scant protection from the cold.

12

I know next to nothing about the widow. Wielemann's diaries only recount the times they were in close proximity, all of which are marked by a voluminous silence.

Should we attribute it to indifference, impotence, or to the idea that the written word is incapable of preserving certain worldly matters and is, as a result, a form of sacrilege or betrayal? Personally, I'm inclined towards the latter hypothesis, but only because it seems inconceivable to me that Wielemann never gave any importance to that woman and her secrets. I'm unable to confirm anything about her family origins, her past, or even the events that left her a widow. I know absolutely nothing about her beyond the hulking responsibility she had hidden away in the attic, a duty that bore all the hallmarks of being a familial labour of love. I'm not even able to say how he came to form part of her life.

I do, however, imagine her standing for long stretches by the window that looked out onto the western plains. From there she might contemplate the fields ready for harvesting, or left unsown due to the war, the patches of emerging weeds, the cottages dotted along the city limits exhaling quivering threads of smoke in the twilight, the modest Sant Bartomeu mountains and the cave at the top where they said witches met and was the source of many childhood memories, the Port del Comte behind it, dark, wide and white-topped, appearing like a reclining giant there to safeguard the solidity, familiarity and continuity of every word and deed, and the evening calmly lowering a veil over it all. And I imagine a man sitting behind her at the table, a strange man who had appeared unexpectedly on her doorstep and who she welcomed into her home because she had no say in the matter and because he didn't seem a bad sort. But the man was a mystery, or more precisely, a silent, opaque mass devoid of anything worth unravelling. He was pure foreignness sitting suddenly by her side. I picture her standing rooted to the spot with all these thoughts swirling around her head before merging into an indistinguishable whole; a life lived without complaints or confessions, a life I'm unable to tell if it was one of submission or a hard-fought form of resistance.

13

Carnival came around like a distant relative appearing out of the blue. While the celebration of sin was alive and well in the rest of Spain, Solsona – a city firmly under the thumb of the legitimate king and the holy church – thought twice before lighting the touchpaper. Could it be celebrated with the same debauchery? Could it be celebrated at all? The city council drew up an edict urging Christian conduct, which the town crier announced in his usual booming voice, leaving the inhabitants to ponder the exact meaning of those words. On Thursday, the first day of Carnival, stifled shouts and giggling could be heard on the frozen streets, while in the large luxury homes a cagey Carnival King held court.

Yet, much like a traveller who first checks the sturdiness of an old bridge before crossing carriage and all, those initial couple of days were, in reality, a test. The bridge held firm and a long line of revellers lost no time in crossing over to the other side. On Saturday and Sunday, vibrant voices began spreading through the darkest corners of the city and the first garishly coloured outfits were seen. By Monday, the taverns were full of candid accounts of the previous day's festivities. On Tuesday lunchtime, Wielemann found an envelope on his pillow. The widow had no idea who had delivered it. He was being invited to a fancy dress party at the grandest of all the stately homes near the Travesset Gate. Coincidentally, it was located at the exact point where the widow's and the doctor's streets converged.

He went to see Foraster, who he found sprawled out on the sofa with all the shutters closed, nursing a headache. Labouring to his feet, he started pulling moth-eaten clothes out of the wardrobe. They ruled out the nondescript clothing that had belonged to his father and a Christino army officer's uniform. When Foraster's grandmother saw what they were up to she went over to show them one of her ample dresses, which Wielemann rejected with a violent shudder. Eventually they came across one of the gowns Foraster wore when working, along with the masks, caps and glasses he used to protect his face from being splattered with blood when carrying out amputations. It was the most sensible option. The doctor agreed to let him borrow the outfit, but on one condition: that he lent him his Prussian uniform.

Feeling slightly ridiculous, Wielemann tip-toed out of the house just as the long shadows began to sneak along the stone walls. The intermittent gusts of wind had him thrusting his hands under his armpits to protect them from the bitter cold. All along the street leading to the Travesset Gate were groups of two or three people ostentatiously dressed and speaking in low voices as if plotting. Wielemann walked straight past without looking at them. He knocked on the door to the huge house and was ushered inside by a maid dressed in lace and sporting cat whiskers. If she had not gently pushed him through the door, he may well have headed straight back home, even more mortified than before.

The same soft hand guided him along a vast corridor shrouded in a mysterious, hazy hue, past portraits of dark, pensive and – owing to the dim light – disproportionate gentlemen. The sensation was one of there being little air, or rather an abundance of it but its heaviness made it impossible to inhale. The hand stopped Wielemann and reached forwards to open a double door.

It took him a while to make out what was in front of him. If it's at all possible to imagine a general yet amorphous movement with only a handful of candles serving as indistinct reference points, it would be that. Or perhaps a kaleidoscopic collision of colour, distinguishable but devoid of outlines. The uproar of voices, excited shouts, whispers, and shrieking surrounded him, almost completely drowning out the uneven and aimless music coming from the barrel piano. Wielemann took a step backwards, bumped into the closed door and desperately searched for a fixed point to focus his eyes upon. To his relief, he saw a dainty individual standing near him wearing a green mask that it was impossible to know what it hoped to represent and Wielemann did his best to adopt the pose of a fellow reveller. The man turned to face him and revealed two damp tentacles attached to his forehead which curved upwards with two balls on the end while he wiggled and gyrated his tongue through a hole in the mask. The slowness with which those snail protuberances emerged seemed contrived to cause an array of reactions, from stupefaction to fascination to disgust.

Abandoning all hope, Wielemann threw himself into the pandemonium. He couldn't tell if the room was large or small, if there were hundreds of people or no more than a dozen. Isolated from the others, intimate spaces opened up between the freakishly dressed bodies, where forbidden acts took place. He found himself opposite a curvaceous woman covered in glistening green scales, her eyes concealed behind a snake mask. She slithered up to him and whispered into his ear with a voice that sounded like smashing glass: 'Have you ssseen His Majesssty the Carnival King?' Wielemann improvised an exculpatory smile and beat a hasty retreat only to collide into a feathery creature with a swivelling head and two enormous, neurotic eyes who was jumping up and down like a flea.

'Word is… there's a foreigner here. What do you know about him? Hey? Hey?'

Wielemann glimpsed a gap between two guests and escaped to a solitary corner and leant against the wall. Everything was still chaos around him. Rather than illuminating the darkness, the tall candles created a chain of tenebrous expanses filled with shifting forms. Wielemann tried to reassure himself by remembering a few basic facts: his name, where he was from, what he was doing there (but the word 'there' clogged up his head and forced him to start all over again). At that moment, a deep, measured voice displaying both rationality and firmness – as though rising from all the remote moments in which humanity could be saved only by forgetting itself – arrived as if to draw him out of his self-absorption. At first, Wielemann couldn't understand a word of what was being said to him, but those sounds soothed him nonetheless. They gradually became clearer and it was as though Wielemann and whatever was giving rise to that voice had distanced themselves from the other beings in the room. Everything was both close by and far off in the distance; they could hear the commotion, yet they were surrounded by silence.

'What a lively evening, wouldn't you agree? Everyone seems so tremendously eager.' Wielemann turned to face the friendly presence: it was a piece of sedimentary rock five cubits high and two cubits wide with horizontal incisions on one side and a protruding stomach held up by two short and skinny legs.

'I'm not sure I'm in the mood for it tonight. I feel hollow. You also look a bit reluctant, if you don't mind me saying. Hang on a moment.'

The rock took a few steps away from Wielemann. When he returned, he reached out a tiny hand and presented him with a *porró* full of wine. Wielemann held the spout to his mouth and drank in desperation.

'I was told there would be a pleasant party here tonight, but all I see is mayhem. A lot of agitation but little joy, wouldn't you agree? Are you a close acquaintance of the master of the house?'

Wielemann continued drinking.

'A rumour's going around that there's a man here tonight from the east, a real character apparently. Greek, I was told, or perhaps Venetian. I haven't seen him. I, for one, like all things foreign. I don't get out much. I'm rather sedentary, you see. But I enjoy hearing all the news from abroad. When the wind blows, I think about all the grains of sand it's carrying from the deserts of Africa and the steppes of Russia, and about all the creatures that have seen those grains and ingested and excreted them. I sense a vibration, nature's pulse beating anew in every moment, a nature that makes the gods, the mountains, the ants, even our sense of pride and shame, wouldn't you agree? And it's always inside of us, just as we are always inside of it. Oh, it makes me crumble with emotion!'

Wielemann dried his lips on his sleeve. The rock edged closer.

'*Excusez-moi, il faut que je m'en aille.*'

The rock, however, continued in a deep, calm voice and an impeccable accent.

'*Ah, vous êtes français!* You know, in Languedoc the rocks are beautiful, in fact…'

Wielemann threw himself head first into the pandemonium once again.

Hours later, a door shut behind Wielemann and the air became less dense. The room, furnished with sofas and low tables, was large but felt cramped owing to a massive fireplace where dozens of sausages were sizzling on a grill. Six men had positioned themselves around the fire: two were lying on the floor pricking the meat, another was leaning against the mantelpiece, while the remaining three were standing around chatting. All six were dressed in brightly coloured robes.

'Well, well, well. If it ain't the Russian.'

Wielemann recognised them instantly. But, apart from a passing glance, the Shambolic Six showed little interest in either him or, by the looks of things, anything else going on around them. One of them was biting into a sausage he was clutching in his fist, whereas another went to great lengths to cut his into thin slices so as not to stain his outfit. The one leaning on the mantelpiece appeared abandoned in a world without thoughts, while the other three spoke in hushed tones with conspiratorial looks. Feeling his head increasingly groggy, Wielemann went to seek refuge on the sofa furthest from them that he could find.

On the armchair opposite him, the snail-man had gently curled up into a ball, indifferent to everything around him, his retractable tentacles vibrating softly with a pure and intense pleasure. The snake was sensually spread out on another sofa, slowly coiling herself around a stunned owl.

'That's the foreigner over there. Strange, don't you think?'

The maid who had opened the front door to Wielemann sat down by his side and plunked a *porró* in his lap. He looked over to the man who had just been pointed out to him, in the middle of the room, but there was nothing particularly strange about him. If anything he looked typically Mediterranean. His face, however, did have a waxy tone, as though made of some inorganic material, which contrasted with the energetic movement of his moustache and his enthusiastic hand gestures. A circle had formed around him composed of two bishops, a priest, a mayor wielding a mayoral rod, a Carlist general and a Liberal lieutenant. He was chattering away, mechanically stringing open vowels together, solely out of the pleasure of hearing himself speak without anyone seemingly able to understand a word he was saying, despite their attempts to conceal the fact behind exaggerated laughter.

'Just look at that. What a way to twitter on.'

'Like a bloody bird.'

'He ain't the Carnival King, is he?'

'That's a Venetian and a Russian we've got in Solsona now. It'll be like Paris here soon, God 'elp us.'

'Didn't they say he was Greek?'

'Greek Catholic.'

'Stranger things have happened.'

'Oh, and that other one ain't Russian, he's Persian.'

'What's this obsession you got with making up words?'

'Where the bleeding hell is the Carnival King anyway?'

'He don't understand a thing, does he? Huh? This little birdy from Venice. What a sight.'

'Yup, sure is.'

The voices buzzed in Wielemann's head like a swarm of bees. He placed the empty *porró* on the floor and curled up on the sofa. The maid snuggled up next to him. The Russian-Persian-French-Prussian-Catholic-non-Catholic felt disorientated and overcome by an all-encompassing fatigue, heavy like a boulder which, after rolling down the mountainside, remains stuck between two oaks, pushes with all its might but remains inert, rests a while, feels its forces fade and finally surrenders. Wielemann was aware of the girl's searching hand but he didn't have the strength to consider it inappropriate. His sight, touch, hearing and sense of smell were dazed, confused, and mixed up. He could touch the rough darkness and see the heavy aromas. Finally, he stopped connecting ideas.

When the maid nudged him awake, he remembered having sat down on the sofa, but he had no idea how long he had been there: five minutes? An hour? Ten? He recognised some of the people in the room: the Venetian-Greek, the two bishops, the mayor, the Carlist general, the Liberal lieutenant, the snail-man, the owl, the snake, the walking rock. There was even a man dressed in a Prussian uniform that looked enormous on him, a short man who couldn't keep still; only after a while did he realise it was Miquel Foraster. A tall woman with long grey hair and a pointy hat had since joined the party along with another woman who, although not appearing to be in fancy dress, had terrifying white eyes that made one want to hide behind the sofa. The Shambolic Six were nowhere to be seen.

Wielemann noted his head was still groggy as the maid offered him another *porró*.

The guests were displaying the first signs that the night was drawing to an end. One of the bishops dropped like a stone onto the sofa while wailing: 'I'm dying!' Everyone laughed, including the bishop. The Carlist general then stood up and imitated him, followed by the woman in the pointy hat. The maid howled with laughter. Miquel Foraster also threw himself down. And the Liberal lieutenant. And the snail-man. And the snake, twisting and turning. One by one, the dead were resuscitated and the circle became infinite. Everyone was standing up, falling down, and laughing. Even Wielemann felt obliged to let himself fall discreetly backwards. The absurd, inebriated laughter intensified and increased until – a jar of flour in one hand and a shaving brush in the other – the maid began whitening the faces of all the authorities, of all the animals, of everyone, while shouting in a burlesque voice: 'Repent!' Finally, the Greek fell theatrically to the floor with a hand on his heart and someone shouted:

'He's the Carnival King!'

They shrouded him with a sheet and carried him to the first room Wielemann had entered that evening, which they found empty, stained with wine and mud, and with all the shutters closed. They left the Greek in the middle of the room and, giggling the whole time, lit long candles, which they placed around him. The cortege then made a circle around the Carnival King and knelt down. The priest, followed by the others, began to recite with solemnity and exaggerated sorrow:

'*Libera nos, Domine, de morte æterna, in die illa tremenda…*'

'Deliver us, O Lord, from death eternal, on that fearful day…'

'*…quando cœli movendi sunt et terra, dum veneris iudicare sæculum per ignem.*'

'…when the heavens and the earth shall be moved, when thou shalt come to judge the world by fire.'

The owl then intervened:

'For he knoweth our frame; he remembereth that we are dust…'

'…as for man, his days are as grass: as a flower of the field, so he flourisheth,' responded the woman in the hat.

The bishops, the mayor, the general and the lieutenant then intoned:

'I am made to tremble, and I fear, till the judgement be upon us, and the coming wrath.'

'*Tremens factus sum ego, et timeo, dum discussion venerit, atque ventura ira.'*

The priest continued, joined by the woman with the fearsome eyes:

'Dies illa, dies iræ, calamitatis et miseriæ, dies magna et amara valde.'

'That day, day of wrath, calamity and misery, day of great and exceeding bitterness...'

'...when thou shalt come to judge the world by fire.'

The maid, the rock, Foraster and Wielemann then formed a choir:

'Requiem æternam dona ei, Domine: et lux perpetua luceat eo.'

'Rest eternal grant unto him, O Lord: and let light perpetual shine upon him.'

Afterwards, a barely audible voice said:

'Do not mourn the Carnival King, for he is destined to return and we are not.'

Perhaps it was tiredness but after more laughter everyone became serious. The priest's yawn infected the rest of the officiants and it spread around the circle. Their eyelids became heavy. The maid dressed in lace, her whiskers smudged all over her face, fell forwards as she nodded off, her forehead coming to rest on the Greek's pale white hand. Her eyes suddenly opened wide and she let out a bloodcurdling scream. 'He's dead! He's dead!' she said with the little air her state of panic allowed her to exhale. Wielemann touched the hand of the man playing the role of the deceased: life had truly departed him. Foraster then walked over to certify it in his professional manner.

Outside, the clock struck midnight with twelve slow, chilling chimes. The priest burnt the pages of his breviary with a candle and spread the ashes on the foreigner's forehead. His voice became richer and softer, like two arms locked in a heartfelt embrace:

'Memento, homo, quia pulvis es et in pulverem reverteris.'

14

It's the first of March and I have less than two months to send the completed translation but barely half of it's finished. Wielemann has taken up too much of my time. I was going to write to the publisher to let him know the translation would be late when I found the following message in my inbox:

Raül,

I can't wait to publish Lichnowsky! Just imagine: I dedicate all my free time to reading about Prussian history just so I can get a taste of his world. It's remarkable to think how that petulant aristocrat was something it's impossible to be nowadays: Prussian.

Amid the ruins of World War II, the Allies signed a decree announcing that: 'the Prussian State together with its central government and all its agencies are abolished.' One sentence erased centuries of perseverance. The preamble justified the decision, affirming that, from its inception, it had been a 'bearer of militarism and reaction.' Prussia was to be the scapegoat for Germany's sins. Henceforth, the evil root severed and the nation purged of blame, Germans could get on with the business of living prosperously. It wasn't such a bad solution when you think about it. It's always more reasonable to abolish a state than to destroy an entire country.

But, in reality, the Allies were only killing a ghost. By then, Prussian territories were Russian, Lithuanian, Polish or Allied occupied. Prussian autonomy had in fact already ceased to exist fifteen years prior when the Reich seized control. But it had died even before then, right after World War I when Wilhelm II abdicated and went into exile in Holland. And before that, when the German Empire was unified. The day before being proclaimed Emperor, Wilhelm I confessed to Bismarck, with tears in his eyes: 'Tomorrow is the unhappiest day of my life. Tomorrow we will bury the Kingdom of Prussia.'

I'm not aware of any state having died on more occasions. And each time it died they accused it of being a dead and soulless apparatus.

But if that wasn't enough, Prussia took its name from an extinct Baltic people. That dead tribe, mutating into its conquerors' state, wandered Europe for centuries like a zombie, waging wars, annexing customs and territories, disciplining, dissolving itself within a larger unit, burying itself over and over again.

So much devastation, Raül.

In short, I'll write to him some other time.

15

When Wielemann got home, his entire body was buzzing with electricity. Driven by the impulse of routine, he hurriedly tucked himself into bed but there was no prospect of his falling asleep, not with all the music, words, and images from earlier that day still hurtling through his head. He had gone with Foraster to witness the opening ceremony at the Carlist university, which happily coincided with the celebrations to mark the monarch's birthday. In the morning, they had endured a solemn service at the Dominican college church along with its teaching body of doctors and scholars, the bishop, the president of the Supreme Junta, the Provincial Governor and a host of moustachioed students within whom drowsiness and instilled decorum were slugging it out in a fight to the death. In the afternoon, during a spirited inaugural speech, a lecturer in jurisprudence had evoked a complete world in which doctrine and praxis were one and the same and where the body's pulsations were transmuted into enlightened faith, as though the pages of a colossal theological summa had spread over the earth and covered every crack and crevice. But it was a world that had given itself over to fire and profanation, folly and contempt, murder and blasphemy. A deranged Liberal, some so-called member of that thing they had christened Parliament, explained the orator, had not had any qualms about conspiring with the devil to prop up his moribund government, even going as far as to proclaim: long live hell and its empire, its power and its doctrines, for God no longer resides in Spain and henceforth we shall govern ourselves according to the instinct of our ideas and passions and thus shall we make the nation happy, we who are men and nothing more than men!, which is no better than saying: we who are base and lecherous and corrupt and anarchic and avaricious and dying, and nothing more! But given events are mere manifestations of ideas, the orator continued, it's imperative for us to rectify them by preaching the good word, for that is how we shall destroy the evil they have cast. 'Allow yourselves to be penetrated, my dear boys, by the illuminating and consoling truth. Purify yourselves of the turpitudes of mind and body, deliver yourselves from the usurping revolutionary government and the harlot who arouses it, revere the venerable and Catholic sovereign Don Charles v, may God protect him, and through him worship the benevolent Lord who pacifies man's pernicious instincts.' The students standing at the back stifled yawns, as impervious to the rhetoric of angels as to that of the devil. Foraster had been smiling throughout. The dissonant notes of a military band brought events to a close and Wielemann rushed off to the doctor's house to play Beethoven and rid himself of the shrill sound still ringing in his ears.

Now in the uniform darkness of his room, the silent night was full of anonymous sounds that came slipping through the gaps in the doors and windows, sounds which, rather than emanating from people or animals or objects, come from a world we are incapable of perceiving during the restlessness of day: a barely audible creak, a piercing and drawn-out screech, a vast and atmospheric chord that rises slowly from the depths, elevates things slightly and then evaporates. With a wholly counterproductive effort, Wielemann closed his eyes and tried to sleep until he heard a different type of sound. It was a prolonged panting which, as it grew stronger, was punctuated by exhaled and exclaimed vowel sounds underscored by thuds, as though the solitary moaning were the last remaining sound after humanity's demise. It only lasted a short while before silence was restored. Afterwards, Wielemann, covered in goosebumps, heard footsteps descend the staircase. Taking as much care as he could, he got out of bed and edged towards the door. Through a gap he could make out the round and ample figure of an unfamiliar woman straightening her clothes. The widow was waiting for her on the bottom step and the unknown woman stopped next to her. The widow then proceeded to hug her for a long time, both tenderly and with gratitude, and only appeared to end the embrace reluctantly as if wanting to hold onto her much longer. She then placed two coins in the woman's hand, which the other accepted with a nod before leaving. Wielemann darted silently back to bed like a little boy caught getting up to no good but awash with an adult anxiety that understood without understanding a thing. He slowed his breathing, closed his eyes and curled up into a ball under the black woollen blanket, desperately trying to recuperate the sounds of the night but his swirling and uncontrollable thoughts kept them out of reach.

He listened to the bell strike twelve, then a quarter past. He could still see the woman descending the staircase, her shapely hips swaying from side to side, but afterwards she vanished and more impersonal yet pulsating sinuosities appeared which rubbed and wrapped around him as he tossed and turned in bed. There were two short, sharp chimes of the bell. Soft cheeks, legs and breasts pressed up hard against him and spread over him, stimulating him, before he sank himself inside. As the bell struck a quarter to, he saw two huge black eyes appear from amid the curves and fix him with their uncomprehending gaze. He got out of bed and went into the hall to sit by the window, his mind free from forms. The timid, waxing moon caressed the lonely world with its rays, but the world, rather than sleeping, remained inert under some fervid pressure. In the fields and along the paths, not a single shadow stirred, but on the horizon the curved lines of the mountains trembled and more sinuous shapes, substantial and superhuman, slipped along the peaks and embraced Wielemann once more. He stood up with a start. Behind him were the widow's huge black eyes and her hesitant, husky breathing. A single toll of the bell paralysed everything for a moment before Wielemann stepped away and closed his eyes. More shapes wrapped around him, warm and irrefutable.

16

Today I finally plucked up the courage.

Joan,

Your e-mail of three weeks ago coursed through my veins, tormented me in my sleep and stalked me for days. I couldn't help but envisage Prussia as an electrified skeleton bolting across Europe while dragging a herd of dwarves behind it. What skeletons are dragging us along?

I must confess that Lichnowsky will be late. Very late. When we see each other next, I'll explain everything that's been going on. That man's world has become too personal; it's burrowed itself under my skin and doesn't allow me to work with a cool head. I'll need a few more months but hopefully it'll be ready after the summer. I'm sorry if this puts you in a tight spot.

I'm sorry. I truly am.
Raül

17

They followed the banks of the River Black, which was little more than a ditch overgrowing with vegetation. All along the water's edge, poplars gradually began to rise amid the tall, resplendent grass, while the other bank was an untamed wilderness of brambles. The shade cast by the thick vegetation wrapped around the two hikers but they could still make out the freshly-sown, serene spring fields beyond the river and the brush. They allowed their eyes to wander high and wide, until a bog or pool forced them to focus on the path in front of them. Soon they left the poplars and the river behind and entered a pine forest whereupon the terrain began to rise steeply and the sun flashed between the trees.

Wielemann followed Foraster's fast stride with his head full of questions. On the surface there was nothing to it: Soler had handed him a 'top secret' envelope and the job of getting it to one Senyor Lleal of Sant Llorenç de Morunys, insinuating that the satisfactory execution of said mission would no doubt prompt the King to take an interest in him. After giving him the envelope, he rubbed his hands together as if having just rid himself of something filthy, and disappeared without another word. Wielemann wondered why he had been singled out for the task. Why, for example, could it not have been charged to someone who at least knew where on God's green earth Sant Llorenç de Morunys was? He also questioned why the authorities had needed more than four months to resolve such a simple request, how he had become embroiled in this bizarre situation and what he would tell his father upon his return to Berlin, if he ever returned. As he began up the rocky slope, already drenched in sweat, these thoughts circled above his head like vultures.

However, at the top of the slope the open countryside greeted him like empires of light or verdant seas. Foraster had thought the trip a wonderful idea and had offered to act as both companion and

guide, as long as they went on foot: 'Forget the animals, man.'
He strode with purpose and only opened his mouth to emit an
exclamation of esteem while pointing towards a hill, field, or a
stone farmhouse. They passed a cluster of houses and, high up
on their right, a half-ruined castle observed them from its privi-
leged position. They trekked through fields, cut through woods,
and edged through brier before Foraster clambered impetuously
up another rocky incline leaving an exasperated Wielemann to
chase after him.

And it was in this spirit that they reached a seemingly endless plain, presenting itself to them like a deep breath suspended
between the hilltops and the ravines or like smooth and sustained
meditation. Instead of losing its equilibrium, the exultant earth
showed itself to be firmer, more accessible, more luminous.
Fields stretched for as far as the eye could see, interspersed only
by the odd house or the static speck of some other traveller, and
looming large in the background was a heavily pockmarked cliff
face. Foraster stopped to catch his breath and smiled proudly.
The barrage of questions that had been hounding Wielemann
faded away. The path in front of them was perfectly flat and they
had the feeling of walking afresh.

'How about telling me a story?'

Though he heard the question, Wielemann didn't answer. Not
out of disinterest, distraction or disdain, but because his inner
mechanism responsible for responding had been deactivated and
the pleasure of being there was so intoxicating and undeniable
that he had become utterly indifferent to interrogations.

'Alright, well I'll tell you one then: the life and death of
Gaietà Ripoll. A full-blooded Carlist like you ought to enjoy
it. Grandpa, may he rest in peace, often talked about him. As
kids they played a lot together. They used to have foot races up
to the springs and return to the city drenched in sweat. When
they got to the Plaça Sant Joan the same thing always happened,
which at first confused and troubled Grandpa: young Gaietà

would kneel before the fountain with its chapel perched on top and cross himself. Certainly no one could ever claim the chapel was capable of provoking intense religious sentiment, but each time without fail Gaietà would kneel down, make the sign of the cross and stay completely silent. Not a single prayer or even a quick amen. He simply crossed himself and kept perfectly still. It was precisely that that struck Grandpa as odd because he'd grown up seeing all sorts of solemn, hysterical, and grotesque gestures along with the usual chaotic jumble of words muttered more in hope than expectation. It was a way of letting it all out, I suppose, or of turning your feelings into something physical, expel them from your body and watch them evaporate into the ether. You played your part in the show and then you could breathe more easily. But not our Gaietà. Oh no. He kept it all locked inside. Two or three times a week, after they'd been running up to the springs in full view of everyone he'd kneel down, cross himself and keep schtum. All the prayers he refused to say out loud he kept inside. As the years passed, Grandpa was left with the impression that Gaietà was made of sterner stuff. Both of them went to seminary school but neither of them became priests. Gaietà, however, had a peculiar way of receiving moral teachings. Whereas his peers would recite the commandments by memory and then poke fun at them out on the quad, he uttered them almost in a whisper, filling his speech with agonising pauses as though searching for them in the most remote depths of his being yet entirely conscious of the gravity of evicting them from their sanctuary. This was a boy of astonishing moral virtue or, more precisely, a boy with an astonishing faith in moral virtue. He strolled serenely past the seminary school toughs and amid the flying stones, the blasphemies and manic howls with a mystical calm that, by all appearances, protected him. Not even when a stone went whizzing past his nose – which didn't happen to him as much as it did to his classmates – did he lose his composure. They'd been taught the importance of turning

the other cheek, but he had no need for that: he just kept on strolling, breathing, and meditating, and left everyone in his path
amazed. Later in life, Gaietà became a doctor. Maybe that's why
Grandpa talked so much to me about him: he must've thought
we were kindred spirits or something. It was probably him who
gave my father the idea of me training to be a doctor. Anyway,
Gaietà didn't change. To Grandpa and everyone else he was still
the same mystifying mix of moral virtue and inner abysses.

'Grandpa and Gaietà both fought against the Frenchman
and, from what I've heard, it was an odd time full of a strange
enthusiasm, as if every pine, beech and oak had uprooted itself of
its own accord and the forests initiated a chaotic crusade against
the standardisation of modern armies. I've no idea if Gaietà ever
felt comfortable amid the violence. I can't imagine he did but,
who knows, maybe he saw a simplicity and sincerity in it that
he also recognised in himself. Your guess is as good as mine.
Instinct's a mystery. Either way, I find it almost impossible to
picture him holding a rifle and spattered with blood, although
no doubt he would mostly have been attending to the wounded.
He was taken captive and ended up in France, where people said
he was infected with and transformed by some type of northern
disease of the mind, but Grandpa didn't buy it. He said, if Gaietà
had indeed changed, it was because he'd concentrated more
on himself and become more single-minded. At most, maybe
he'd found confirmation of a few things in books. Eventually,
Gaietà returned home and had a long career in the military
where he displayed an almost unheard of level of discipline.
What happened next didn't strike Grandpa as strange. In fact,
he was one of the few who it didn't surprise. Either he upped
and quit the army or they threw him out because suddenly he
went down to Valencia to work as a schoolmaster. A lot of folk
from Solsona end up there and are often successful, but in the
case of this man it's hard to use words like success and failure.
Given it was Gaietà's conduct and how he handled himself that

was so impressive, I imagine that was the main content of his lessons. Grandpa had no doubt the children learnt to read and write, to add and subtract, and he was sure they did it fairly well too, but the children learnt something more: there was an alternative way of being, more silent, more intense, which had no need for Catholic pomp. Gaietà spoke to them of a God who was all around them and who the students would discover in their hearts if they would only learn to purify themselves from within and carve open a forgotten, feared and often ridiculed space. There they were to build their abode, furnish it with sincere thoughts and incorrupt feelings, contemplate them joyfully for hours on end, become accustomed to them and worship the hidden essence of a God who was everywhere and only hid away when the priests performed their exaggerated rituals. He even told them it wasn't necessary to go to Mass or to say their Hail Marys. The children were confused and fascinated in equal measure, but their parents were terrified; some were in a state of out-and-out panic. However, when they went to confront him, they were received with his usual disarming calmness. They insisted for days on end, one of them even threatened to kill him, before finally they went about ostracising him: they ignored him in the street, the baker stopped selling him bread and someone even threw a stone through his window. But Gaietà didn't say a word. He was furnished with a higher reason, softer than human skin. A number of parents stopped taking their children to school but when they went out to play they'd spot Gaietà out in the fields and realise he was even stranger and more sentimental when surrounded by nature. He explained the importance of loving the trees, the corn, the grasshoppers, the worms, the earth under their feet, all of God's creations, whether alive or dead, real or make believe. Each child was to invite into their enormous inner sanctuary some despised creature, give it refuge, care for it, and worship the God in it. Charity was the only way of breaking through the dams of civilisation, the only way of giving yourself fully to the justice of love, even if that meant coming into conflict with laws, churches, kings, and customs. It carried on like that for a year, two at the most, before he was arrested, not by the State but by an ecclesiastic tribunal, a type of Inquisition: the fearsome Junta of Faith led by the diocese of Valencia. They locked him in a prison cell and ordered him to officially recognise Catholic dogma. That was in the year of our Lord 1824.'

Strolling through the plain, it was impossible not to feel the urge to sprint in all directions and delight in the open space. The sun, rising steadily in the sky, began to warm them.

'Grandpa, by now terminally ill, found what happened next even less of a surprise. Every day, a priest was sent to remind him of the Catholic Church's benevolence and tolerance. I don't know if anyone else – more methodical and, er, good with their hands – was sent too. But the fact of the matter is, when the priest observed him, he was struck by the man's tenderness and tranquillity and, after the first few days, rather than trying to indoctrinate him, they began to talk in earnest. Gaietà spoke to him of a God who, despite being his, was everywhere and the priest, understanding perfectly, was at times close to tears but he always made a point of reminding the prisoner that charity also meant respecting our neighbours' traditions and rituals which, regardless of their worthlessness or unimportance, help us mark a path through life. Charity meant being tolerant of other people's customs for the simple reason that they belong to them. It meant freeing oneself of the arrogance of having discovered the truth and learning to be humble among the meek. No doubt there were moments when Gaietà agreed but he stuck to his guns, telling the priest that God was in everything and everyone and that he would never bow before His usurpers. The priest looked at him tearfully, quite possibly understanding more than Gaietà realised, while taking pity on the lost sheep. At the end of each long session, a secretary would enter the cell with a declaration of faith in the One, Holy, Catholic and Apostolic Church and ordered Gaietà to sign it. But each time he refused.

'He never did sign it. The same sequence of spiritual conversations, demands, resistance and – who knows – torture dragged on for two years. 'You can lead a horse to water...' was what Grandpa always said about Gaietà. He liked that saying and used it a lot. While the prisoner's unshakable pride saddened the priest, he came to love him dearly. He implored him to lie, to scribble under the declaration of faith and go off and live in some peaceful place far from everything and everyone. But Gaietà had made a firm decision: under no circumstances would he defile himself with falsities and expel God from his inner temple. He made it clear his answer was and always would be no, and that no amount of suffering would make him go back on his word. He was sentenced to burn at the stake. The tearful priest begged his superiors to show mercy on the lost sheep and, to their credit, they weren't completely insensitive to his pleas: instead of being burnt alive, he was to be hanged above a barrel decorated with symbolic flames. People turned up in their hundreds to watch. There was no last-minute reprieve, of course, and Gaietà Ripoll's feet, sporting the espadrilles of his native city, the same he used to wear when sprinting through the fields of Solsona with Grandpa, swung in the middle of Valencia's Plaça del Mercat. How did the public react? Did they clap and cheer, hurl insults, shrink back in fear, faint...? I really don't know. The truth is, I can't even begin to imagine something like that.'

The open highland stretching out before them fell into darkness as Wielemann recalled the cries of: "Long live the Spanish Inquisition!" the day of his arrival. He had never had any staunch convictions like Gaietà Ripoll but he had known many Prussians who did. Three words, laden with shame, formed in his mouth and he was only able to force them out with considerable effort:

'The Inquisition... fanaticism...'

'Whoa, there! Hold your horses! I dare say I'd agree with you if you hadn't gone racing ahead of me. That's how most of Europe saw it, anyway: the cruel dogmatism of a medieval ecclesiastical tribunal clashing with the free spirit of modern man, old faith against new reason, tradition versus liberty. I enjoy reassuring frameworks, I really do. They make the world a more beautiful place. But, alas! Events are much more cynical and perverse than we like to admit, and they spit in the face of our moral frameworks. In reality, the poor, desperate priest, the sinister individual who entered every evening with the declaration of faith, the ecclesiastics, bishops, and illiterate lay brothers were only asking one thing of Gaietà, one simple, utterly meaningless thing: a scribble on a page full of formulaic phrases. In other words: write his name and go on believing whatever he pleased. To be honest, apart from the priest, I don't think any of them gave two hoots about Gaietà's private thoughts. That inner temple of his, upholstered with fine and elegant theology, left them entirely indifferent. In fact, I'd go as far as saying he hardly even existed to them. They weren't demanding a complete inner conversion or spiritual transformation, merely a gesture. Freedom for the price of a scribble. Nothing more. Yes, I grant they were cynics, but I don't see how they were any more cynical than the majority of people I've ever known. Or do you hope to go through life entering into each and every heart and analysing its deficiencies and triumphs before passing judgement? Why, it would be unbearable, not to mention the end of civilisation. Even if that mob of hierarchs wasn't aware of all that, it sure acted like it was. But not Gaietà, oh no. Gaietà had found the truth. Gaietà was genuine, graceful and proud like all true believers. That's why he couldn't be reconciled with the Catholic Church. When they sentenced him, it was cynicism condemning faith. And which of the two, I ask you, is modern and which is old?'

'But… his feet swinging…'

'Heinous… inexcusable… sickening, even. But so easily avoided…'

'I don't know, principles…'

'Exactly. It's always a question of principles.'

They entered the Cap del Pla tavern, sat down and were immediately served sausages and slices of toasted bread fresh from the fireplace. They ate in silence while relishing the flavours, eyeing the women servers and listening to the music of the conversations around them. An almost palpable ray of sunlight shone through the windows and Wielemann felt brighter, even going as far as to allow himself the liberty of openly expressing his pleasure. Foraster smiled at him.

'Did you come to fight this war on principle?'

'Well, as a matter of fact…'

With their stomachs satisfied, the steep slopes became less sapping. The path rose and narrowed as it followed the mountain ridges between clusters of pine trees and shrubs, and the sky seemed closer and more solid. The peaks to their right, instead of sloping downwards, formed an abrupt conglomeration of cliffs so smooth they seemed to have been sculpted and plunged vertically into the dark depths. Wielemann had never seen anything even remotely like it. He fixed his eyes on the ground in front of his feet to stop his head from spinning. Foraster strolled along the cliff edge and Wielemann, a bag of nerves, watched him from a safe distance. He edged towards the precipice but only to confirm the advantages of staying well away and he imagined himself slipping, sliding and then slamming into the rocks below, his back broken and his leg mangled. Then he pictured the doctor taking out a gouge and cutting through his limb out of pure altruism while jets of blood drenched his overalls. A sudden convulsion made him lurch forwards and he went scampering away from the cliff edge and planted his feet firmly on the ground: if his head spun out of control at least his body would be firm enough to save him. Foraster sent the occasional stone tumbling down the rockface.

'There! Over there!' he said while pointing towards a deep gorge.

Foraster waited a while before doing or saying anything more. Despite having decided to keep his interventions to a minimum, reasoning that if some tragedy had to occur the best he could do was make sure he wasn't to blame, Wielemann would have preferred some form of conversation to the silence, thus he felt a great sense of relief when Foraster finally spoke.

'Those gorges tell another story. This was all plains, once upon a time. Vilabona, they called it, or Fair Lands. One day, Our Lord and Saviour Jesus Christ was walking through here, barefoot, nothing but the tattered clothes on his back, going from door to door begging for alms. It was winter and the fog smothered the trees and houses. Each household turned the vagrant away, perhaps on account of his red hair, who knows, but not before giving him a piece of their mind: "Oi! Piss off out of here, fleabag!", "Don't let me catch you round here again, you son of a bitch!", "Worthless piece of shit. Ain't you got no home to go to?" However, when he knocked on the door of the last house on the edge of town, it inched open to reveal a spindly, stooping old woman who chewed her gummy words before spitting them out. No sooner had the red-headed beggar asked her for a little charity than the woman turned and shouted at her husband to come at once because there was a stranger at the door. The old man, who never understood a word his wife was saying to him given he was as deaf as a post, merely assumed his eldest son had come home early from Sant Llorenç, wondering with his usual ill humour what all the fuss was about. Feeling her blood run slightly cold, the old woman let the Lord in. The younger son, his wife, their children, and the old man were having supper but when the latter saw the tramp's shock of knotted red hair and his filthy rags, well, it put the fear of God into him. He shot to his feet, shuffled slowly backwards and bumped into the wall, leaving his bowl of steaming onion soup on the table. The Lord took it as though they were offering him a meal and a bed for the night. The only house that had offered him shelter, the only house where there was true Christian love! He sat in the old man's chair and began to eat while the old couple watched on in horror and the rest of the family continued with their supper in silence. The Lord looked each one in the eye and said: "Good people". One of the grandchildren stifled a giggle and the daughter-in-law snorted with derision. One by one they went excusing themselves from the table, first the grandchildren, then the son and his wife and, finally, the old woman, all of them retiring to their rooms for the night. The only two that remained were the Lord, busy gathering up and eating all the breadcrumbs, and the old man, still glued to the wall. As he began to slowly slide away, the red-headed visitor went over to the window and hollered: "You might be Vilabona now, but you'll soon be Vilamala!" In other words, Fair Lands was destined to become Bad Lands. He gazed at the old man with saintly wonder and nodded, as though wishing to recognise in him something that hadn't, at any point, occurred to the poor, unwilling host. The old man scurried off to his bedroom, wedged a chair against the door and barricaded himself behind as much furniture as he was physically capable of dragging but he was unable to fall asleep. He was far too aware of the presence of that undesirable sprawled out next to the fireplace doing goodness knows what and he cursed his son who, instead of talking business and getting sloshed in Sant Llorenç, could have had the decency to have come home a day earlier and thrown that intruder out on his ear.

That night, a terrifying crashing sound tore through the darkness for hours. The following morning, our Lord and Saviour had vanished. The family went to look for him in the field when the fog had begun to thin and you can imagine the shock they had when they found the plains completely gutted and ripped apart. All the houses and their inhabitants had been hurled into that hellish hole now serving as a mass grave. Every so often, a few rocks would roll and skip down the steep banks before being swallowed up by the void. The old couples' welcoming home was the only one in the whole town to escape destruction.' Foraster then pointed towards the other side of the gorge. 'That's the house there. Sòbol, was its name.'

Wielemann looked at it for no more than a couple of seconds before fixing his eyes on the ground again. Two dozen crows circled above them and then landed further up the path, hopping and flapping their wings. Emitting a cry of excitement and anticipation, the doctor ran over to see what had caught their attention. His arrival sent the crows scattering in all directions but no succulent carrion or stunned animal was revealed, neither on the path nor the slopes. Nothing. It was as if the birds had been pursuing a ghost. Foraster stopped and looked out over the cliff edge. Wielemann went and stood next to him and immediately had the sensation that the cliffs were inflating, mounting one another and tumbling down. He sat on the ground.

By the time Wielemann stood up again, Foraster had already advanced a significant distance. The path curved as it followed the edge of the ravine and then began to weave its way upwards, leaving the deep chasms hidden from view. Opting for the path less travelled, the doctor scrambled up a rocky slope dotted with patches of vegetation and was soon nowhere to be seen, his invisible presence confirmed only by the occasional thud of a falling rock. Wielemann attempted to follow him but the going was tough and he slipped, clutched desperately around him to stop himself from falling, lost his balance, looked fruitlessly for his friend, continued as best he could, slipped again, lost his breath and felt his legs tremble. He looked up and saw a tall and menacing rockface full of cavities like empty eye sockets and, in the background, the bulging cliffs of Vilamala, above which a lone bird was gliding with unearthly calm between two abysses. Distracted by these images, Wielemann had not noticed the terrain begin to descend and he once again slipped, not because of the loose rocks like before, but because the slope was completely smooth and offered nothing for him to grab on to. He managed to get himself into a sitting position and began to slide along on his backside over a rapidly-moving rivulet of pebbles that gathered pace, leaving him with no time to determine whether two fast approaching trees should be a source of calm or concern. Before he reached them, a large protruding rock brought him to a violent stop. He looked up to find two black, uncomprehending eyes, underneath a pair of large ears and two fragile horns, staring back at him from behind the trees. Wielemann responded with his own stupid gaze and hours could have passed without a single thought forming behind those two pairs of eyes plunged into a panting, sweating amnesia. The beast departed with difficulty as if it were decrepit. Wielemann stood up but with his first step went sliding down the slope, only this time much faster and he desperately tried to repel the mixture of anger, pain, fatigue, and confusion churning inside him because of what he had seen or thought he had seen. Nevertheless, deciding upon surrender as the best form of protest, he stopped struggling and was soon slumped at the bottom of the slope like a sack of potatoes. Foraster looked at him with surprise like someone who has just witnessed something strange but, ultimately, of little importance. Wielemann couldn't figure out how the doctor had managed to appear like that, considering he had climbed much higher, but he preferred to let it go.

The path forked and, after a sharp turn, rose and ran along the ridges again. Foraster turned towards Wielemann and pointed: 'That's the way to Sant Llorenç.' A sense of bemusement began to form inside the panting Prussian's bruised body, followed by an attempt at anger but he lacked the energy for it. The cliffs were now directly to their right but Wielemann kept his eyes firmly on the path as it weaved around rocks the colour of bone piercing the grass like open fractures. As the two hikers ascended, it was as if the whole world had stooped and hid itself under their feet. They eventually came to a plateau, which they contemplated side by side, chimerical in its vastness, like a priceless possession misplaced among the peaks. In the middle of the meadow were the crumbling walls of Sòbol gradually transforming into nature amid the altruistic embraces of the long grass. The doctor sprinted off with a child's enthusiasm but Wielemann, while feeling the urge to follow suit, exercised restraint.

As Foraster ran towards the twisted oak trees at the far end of the meadow, Wielemann lay down on the grass, stretched out his arms and began to float in the deep blue of the sky. The doctor's excited shouts drifted over to him beneath a high, dazzling sun. Wielemann felt warmth above him and coolness below, as though he himself were generating the world's opposing forces or channelling them through his organism. He had the notion that all of his memories had been manufactured for the sole purpose that he would come to lie in that exact spot in that exact moment. Time was neither linear nor cyclical. Time had ceased to exist.

Two hours later, they reached the stone walls of Sant Llorenç. Three unwelcoming and ill-humoured men looked them up and down but when Foraster went over to ask for directions they continued talking as if he weren't there. It was the baker's wife who eventually told them where the house was.

Standing in front of Senyor Lleal's residence, Foraster and Wielemann turned and stared at each other doubtfully and it was the Prussian who made the first move. He stepped forwards and knocked on the low, narrow door but there was no answer. He tried again and the sound of someone swearing and grumbling made them wait more patiently. When the door finally opened, they were greeted by an extremely large woman who, on first sight, seemed incapable of passing through the door. Wielemann concentrated hard so as not to mess up what he was to say:

'A… message… from Solsona… for… Senyor Lleal.'

'I'll give it to him… if I bloody well feel like it!'

Half way through her answer – uttered with a stinging was-pishness, as though she were spitting out some insect that had flown mistakenly into her mouth – the door slammed shut.

Wielemann felt suddenly overwhelmed by an immense and crushing fatigue.

18

At once ethereal and solid, friendship is a strange phenomenon. It's the least natural, least instinctive, least biological of loves and while our continued survival as a species doesn't depend on it, it's something that fills that survival with meaning. Friends emerge out of a shared enthusiasm and this rare affinity isolates them in an immense solitude, allowing them to savour the fecundity of a present that can so often be soured by the past. This is much more valuable than the help they supposedly give one another; on the contrary, between true friends, favours are a source of embarrassment and are forgotten in the act. Friendship is a form of secession, even revolt.

Despite this word not appearing once in Wielemann's diaries, I'm convinced that he and Foraster were true friends, whether or not they had time to explore their wounds and their memories in depth. It was a virginal friendship, both innocent and full of startling discoveries, one of those budding friendships that people occasionally mock with crude or taunting remarks. Neither was searching for the other when their paths crossed, giving each one the fortune of being able to marvel at the other's existence. In a different country, in a different time, their relationship would have likely continued to grow. But friendship is a form of secession, even revolt, and this, of course, can be dangerous if it appears in the middle of a war.

19

He had hardly left the house since his return two days ago. His legs were sore, he wished only to rest and read, and the black eyes appeared before him repeatedly. The widow was almost never around. On the first day she had had his supper waiting for him on the table before immediately making herself scarce and the following day he had also only seen her momentarily. Wielemann loafed around the house, reading in bed or on the window seat, and waited. He wasn't waiting for anything specific; in fact, if she had been there, quite possibly he would have been the one to up and leave. But he waited all the same, perhaps more for the pleasure of having something to wait for, however ill-defined or inexistent. While he waited, he heard moans come from upstairs again, only this time they were miserable and lengthy and accompanied by the occasional crash of some object falling to the floor. But, after so many months of living under that roof, these sounds seemed almost part of the furniture. More than once he had wished to investigate where they were coming from, but the widow's presence and his own apprehension barred him. If one of these noises sprang up while they were having lunch, she would pretend not to have heard it and, when he looked at her in a confused, inquiring manner, she would avert her gaze, wait a little and take her leave. Up until then, Wielemann had regarded it as just another of the city's many mysteries, but now he found himself more alone and even more unoccupied than usual and told himself that the widow's house was, by now, enough his own home to warrant him taking a good look around. He climbed the stairs to the attic.

The first thing he saw as he opened the door was a supernatural light suspending everything in a state of grace: the stillness of a hoop and an eyeless doll propped side by side against the wall, rings of different sizes and colours, circles drawn with imprecision but repeated with geological patience, odd pieces of junk and broken furniture that served no purpose and specks of shimmering dust particles arriving from distant worlds.

At the back of the room was a straw mattress with two large cushions and, in the middle, a small table and two chairs. Sitting with its back to the window and outlined by the soft light, someone with enormous, dark eyes, a flat nose and pro-truding lips drenched in drool was watching him with a perfectly symmetrical face frozen in a broad smile.

The creature's age and curious, amenable gaze were an enigma but it was one Wielemann was determined to solve. Taking a decisive step forwards, however, the mysterious being uttered two indecipherable syllables with an intonation that plunged from high to low like a faulty foot pump. It was at that exact moment Wielemann knew the word for what was sitting before him. He thought about all those months he had lived below without knowing a thing, about the plump, well-endowed woman of the night coming down from the attic, about the widow's exa-ggerated silences, her caresses and her tender touch. He asked himself just how this person was related – because related, he undoubtedly was – to the widow and how exactly she had been left with such a formidable burden.

In Wielemann's day and age, the man staring back at him would no doubt have been labelled a moron, an idiot or an imbecile. After years opting for words such as mongoloid or retarded, today we would likely prefer to call him mentally disabled and we will continue to use this expression until it no longer flatters us and we are forced to find another.

Laden with layers upon layers of thick, oily shadows, the vacant smile called out and clung to him like an embrace, which he did his utmost to repel. Feeling ashamed yet not knowing exactly why, Wielemann hung his head and began to creep away, desperately wanting to distance himself from that violent amalgamation of light and shadow.

Hearing someone coming up the stairs, his body became paralysed at the precise moment when his will was urging him to run and hide and he was left suspended in an enforced disequilibrium. The door opened to reveal the widow. She looked first at Wielemann and then over at the man before clutching the door so fiercely that the ligaments and veins in her arm became clearly visible and her eye began to twitch uncontrollably. Wielemann felt guilty, not for having entered the attic without permission, but for having cornered her, causing her such extreme and evident unease. The widow inadvertently turned her face away with a downward slant, undoubtedly no longer even perceiving what was in front of her, feeling only the anguish caused by time moving implacably onwards and a world that refuses to end once and for all. Wielemann trembled inside, deeply despising the moment, and possibly the widow would have turned, gone back downstairs and shut herself in her room, or he would have felt obliged to say something, anything, however stupid and ungrammatical, or perhaps they would have hugged and felt more isolated than ever. But what happened next meant all that could be avoided.

The man began to sing. It was a slow, uninterrupted whine, both nasal and off key, that attempted to imitate a popular melody. The notes slipped over one another and sank despondently before rising swiftly again to culminate in a resounding, prolonged chord which, after a noisy and hurried intake of breath, began to fray and unravel just like before. I have no idea if the song was sad or celebratory, or even if it was meant to express anything.

The widow let go of the door, walked slowly over to the man and sat down by his side. Taking his hand in hers, she hugged him and began to stroke his forehead. At that point, she stared directly at Wielemann with a look that was neither defiant nor beseeching but which merely informed him that this is how things were.

Once again, Wielemann wondered how old that man-child

could be. Judging by his physique, he must have been around the same age as him, that is to say, between twenty-five and thirty but his complexion had an infantile quality, as if time had stood still for him. Wielemann thought how the widow was old enough to be the man's mother and then the thought flashed through his head that she was, therefore old enough to be his too. The distance between him and the table grew even wider while the widow went on holding the man's hand as he continued to croon. Having grown up flanked by his mother's detached benevolence and his father's absent severity, he had never had to shoulder a single burden in his life and he now felt distinctly embarrassed. Not even in the midst of this invisible war that he was theoretically participating in had he been required to do anything even remotely worthy of mention. At first, those two people by the table provoked little, if any, emotion in him but he soon considered that patronising and paternalistic and so made an effort to regard the scene as a slice of life like any other, without making value judgements, convinced that was the best way to see it. Nevertheless, the grief that had been perched perilously above his head now plunged with all its weight and crushed his high-minded thoughts. Wielemann stared at the floor before slinking out the door and down the stairs.

That same afternoon, he decided to walk over to Foraster's house. He passed the robust, timeless old woman sitting next to the bubbling pot and surrounded by sour-smelling shadows as pungent as they were profuse. The living room was empty and the only sound was the cavernous ticking of the clock. A crumpled copy of *The Constitutional* lay discarded on the armchair and Wielemann went over to pick it up, curious and more than a little alarmed to find a Liberal newspaper in that house of all places. It was an old edition, from August of the previous year, but the headlines could still be made out: 'Absolute power wielded by King of Prussia and Emperor of Austria', 'Impossibility of Catalonia ever declaring independence', 'Municipal budgets'.

Wielemann apathetically left the paper where he had found it, sat down in another armchair, and waited. With the fire still unlit, the only light and warmth that reached him came from the kitchen, limping and weary. The ticking continued at an irritating volume prompting him to stand up and think about leaving, however, passing by the empty piano stool, he changed his mind. Notes from Beethoven's last sonata began to form under his fingers, at first solitary and suggestive, then becoming stronger and multiplying before rising up mutually with meaning and, soon enough, it wasn't so much he who played the piano but the music that had infiltrated and begun to vehemently command him, making him jump and stretch and lurch until he finally lost himself and became just another voice in the counterpoint, as corporeal as the others.

When his fingers came to rest at the end of the movement, Wielemann felt the presence of someone in the room. It was Foraster, flooded with so much emotion by the music that he was unable to speak. Wielemann didn't take up the second movement and instead went to sit silently opposite his equally silent friend, already noting the music loosen the millstone around his neck. The clock filled the room with its deep, sharp ticking and Wielemann noted his throat was terribly dry. The doctor went into the kitchen and came back with a *porró* and two glasses as the pale light of the slow day slinked through the windows. Despite wanting to, Wielemann decided not to say anything, until he couldn't wait any longer and the words exploded from his mouth like a cork from a bottle and he began to talk and talk and talk. He talked about the old and the new, he wove his words into a lifeline and placed it in the doctor's open hands, feeling an immense gratitude, despite everything. They spoke as only true friends can: with words that make sense solely to them, in an atmosphere imperceptible to anyone external, forging an intimate and irrevocable secession.

20

My editor's silence had me worried. He was yet to answer my e-mail from over a month ago but I didn't dare write to him again and instead continued working on Lichnowsky with a deep sense of embarrassment. With the first draft of the translation almost ready to send, today I received the following message:

Dear Raül,

This is Mercè, Joan's wife. Sorry for using his e-mail to write to you but lately our lives have been turned upside down and I'm doing all I can so it doesn't completely fall apart.

For about a month and a half now, Joan has barely left the sofa. The company he worked for has closed down and, at fifty-three years old, he's out of a job. You're already well aware that, when it comes to books, Joan is capable of taking on the most outlandish projects but at his proper job he was no more than a simple, obedient clerk who kept his nose clean. He doesn't even know where to begin to find work. I look for things like mad but it's not easy.

As you can imagine, the publishing house will be closing its doors. He was talking about publishing everything he had lined up but then I reminded him about the bills, the mortgage and the rest. I'm sure Joan will try his level best to pay you as soon as he can but the book, for the time being, will have to be shelved. I'm sorry, Raül, but there's nothing else we can do.

Best of luck,
Mercè

If laptops didn't exist, I would have made a bonfire out of all those pages of translated words and it may well have been one of celebration, too. Either way, there are no more excuses now. I must throw myself body and soul into telling Wielemann's story to the bitter end.

21

The time has come to explain how they set about destroying themselves.

Three twists of fate signalled the end, the first of which is a little-known, half-baked event from dubious sources that I only came across thanks to an archivist with a penchant for local history. The second is well documented and known by anyone remotely interested in the first wave of Carlism. The third and final twist, however, I discovered among Rudolf von Wielemann's diaries.

If there was one enduring entity that all Carlists were to revere, it was the Church, and if there was one person in the city who embodied it, it was the Bishop. But the man assigned this role, a certain Juan José de Tejado from La Rioja, and the responsibility of safeguarding episcopal authority from the threats posed by civil power and war, has left almost no trace in the history books. I picture a man unable to sleep yet desperately tired of conspirators, armed priests speaking in a strange dialect, and University of Cervera lecturers drunk on theology. One June morning, as he contemplated the city from his palace, he saw nothing but an undisturbed emptiness impregnated with a troubling silence, leaving him with the impression that even God had skipped town. He meditated on the mysteries of Providence: how much fortune would it have taken for him to have been sent to a peaceful diocese, far from the infernal racket of the rifles, where he might have been able to dedicate himself to composing beautiful sermons that served no purpose and to collecting prints of the Virgin Mary? If only the Lord might occasionally turn a blind eye to man, if only the world spun differently for him, if only... He looked out over the ramshackle roofs, full of nesting pigeons and hopping birds, miraculously resisting coming crashing down like a house of cards and, beyond them, the wide expanse of vineyards and ploughed fields. Further still, he spied the outline of the austere pine trees basking, far from man, amid spring's finished masterpiece. Tejedo stared misty-eyed while the chatter of a group of guerrillas wafted up to him from the street below, none of whom had any qualms when it came to taking the Lord's name in vain. Rubbing his eyes, he was suddenly overcome by the desire to lose himself in the woods a while. Mounting his mule, he left the palace with the idea of observing the ruins as he crossed the city and then slowly making his way through the trees.

At that precise moment, Father Tristany was coming down Sant Miquel Street sitting high upon his horse. It was quite the spectacle and never before had so much joy been seen surging through one man's body. His instinctive trust in the material proofs of Catholicism had granted him a completely carefree existence, enabling him to live purely for the pleasures of eating and waging war. Had he been handed the chance of living his life over again in any way he chose, he would have opted (presuming he had understood the question put to him) to be born again at the Tristany family home and to maraud through his native land with a pair of musketoons and a rosary, ransacking villages and burning Liberals. Propelled by the exuberance of a life lived to the full, each one of these certainties came blustering down the smooth stones of the sloping street. It was difficult to stop at the best of times, and so it proved for Tristany.

His horse came nostril to nostril with the Bishop's mule, reared up and frantically kicked its front legs. Right there, whether resulting from the physical blow or the moral impact, and possibly accompanied by a sense of relief, Tejado breathed his last.

I picture the Shambolic Six happening to pass by at that exact moment and witnessing the whole thing. They make a circle around the dead man while Father Benet watches on without a single word like someone passing the scene of some unfortunate accident which doesn't affect them and which they couldn't have done anything to prevent. 'He's snuffed it,' they whisper to one another. 'He's snuffed it,' they repeat with bright eyes infused with a mixture of stupefaction and euphoria. 'He's snuffed it!' they shout as they begin to laugh and jump and clap with nervous excitement before remembering that it's not the done thing and their faces become solemn, their movements subdued and, soon enough, they have a sincere sense of the seriousness of death. When more people arrive, they begin to speak in hushed tones but with secret exhilaration, for it's not every day you see a twist of fate of such magnitude.

The full name of the second twist of fate is Roger-Bernard-Charles d'Espagnac, de Couserans, de Comminges and de Foix, Cabalby d'Esplas, Orbesan and Dupac, although he's better known by the adopted and celebrated name of the Count of Spain. A source of rumours and anecdotes like few people in the history of humanity, he was born in a Gascony castle overlooking the River Garonne the day of the Assumption of the Virgin Mary in the year of our Lord 1775. When, in Paris, the heads of people with much less ostentatious names than his began to roll, his family declared war on this new religion infusing plebeians with superhuman strength. His father took him over the Pyrenees to Spain to fight for the restitution of the world and it was in Mallorca where Charles married a robust and restorative name: Dionísia Rossinyol de Delfa i Comellas. After winning every possible military decoration in the fight against revolutionaries and liberals, Ferdinand vii granted him the title of *grande de España*, along with the position coveted by sadists up and down the kingdom: Captain General of Catalonia. It was at that point when his fame as a ferocious and blood-thirsty terrorist really took off; he signed execution orders indiscriminately and with passion, and it was neither here nor there whether his victim was a so-called Liberal dreaming of a constitution or a proto-Carlist more royalist than the King. It was also around this time when rumours of his neurasthenia began to surface.

The twist of fate came in 1838 when this mentally unstable man of sixty-two, having fled the French Revolution as an absolutist yet who had a fondness for executing other absolutists, was appointed to lead the Catalan absolutists in their war effort. However, we do know that it was a difficult and highly contested decision. The responsibility for filling the vacancy fell to the Superior Junta, which was composed of two opposing groups: those who had interests and those who had ideas, that is to say, aristocrats and opportunists versus scholars and fanatics. The Count of Spain was appointed thanks to the former, leaving the latter to bite their tongues but, as we shall see, not for long.

In July of that year, the Count returned from exile in France and set about modernising the Carlist army. In other words, he disciplined it, and any officer unable to obey orders was unceremoniously removed. Father Benet was a victim of this battle between icy intellect and burning passion. Espagnac's aristocratic sophistication and formalist rigour was the antipathy of Tristany's savage, earthy instincts and, whereas the Count was an exile with nothing but a king, the clergyman had nothing but a deep-rooted, sprawling farmhouse filled with rifles, kegs and cured sausage. Stripped of his position, Tristany now departs these pages, just as he would later depart his native land. The new war that was commencing, composed of modern tactics and discipline, wasn't for him. At the end of the day, what's the point of fighting for the past or the permanence of the present if it meant making a load of miserly calculations like a Liberal?

Ironically, the first challenge facing the elegant aristocratic exterminator was the defence of Solsona, the city conquered by Father Benet to both his and the enemy's surprise. Less than a half day's walk from his family home and birthplace, it was where he had learnt macaronic Latin, the basic tenets of Catholicism, and the many, many pleasures of life.

That summer, the Count's new army – modernised as far as circumstances allowed – remained inert while the Liberals continued to conquer territory. The Count stood staring at the horizon, lost in contemplation as the breeze ruffled his white hair, before ordering his troops to burn the woods, crops and Carlist farmhouses lest the enemy get their hands on any of it. Any soldier failing to comply first had their hand chopped off, then their head, before finally being quartered and their limbs left at crossroads along the highway. The Count appeared willing to act right up to the very limits of his power but also to wash his hands of it at a moment's notice. During one particular battle, while his divisions were sweating blood out on the field, the Count didn't give a single command: he had been detained by the visit of a certain young lady close to his heart. Slowly but surely, the first few members of the Superior Junta, aristocrats just like him who had originally endorsed him, began leaving discreetly for France. There was no let up to the Liberal advance and the bad blood only worsened, a situation not helped by rumours that Espagnac had held secret talks with parliamentarians. The Carlists limped from one defeat to another before the Junta finally decided to put an end to the Count's absurd terror. Once dismissed, he was escorted towards Andorra along the moonlit mountain paths of an autumnal Urgellet under the pretext of protecting him from his enemies. His escorts slowly vanished into the night, leaving Espagnac, bereft of his military uniform, to follow the River Segre with only his panting mule and tight-lipped guide for company. Two men coming the other way set upon him, beating him within an inch of his life, and at the first bridge they came to – the aptly-named Pont d'Espia, or Spy's Bridge – strangled him, robbed him of everything he had and threw him into the river with a rock tied to his feet. 'I pushed her in where she would drown and watched my love go floating down' rang out in the damp cold of night. Afterwards, they spread the story that the Count had arrived safe and sound in France, but the days passed and suspicions grew. Unfortunately for the perpetrators of the crime (including its mastermind, the former parish priest of Castelltort de Guixers, Narcís Ferrer), the forces of nature can be entirely unpredictable for, just a few hours after the murder, the rain began to pour intensely and without respite. The Segre swelled and raged like never before but its torrential waters caressed Espagnac's corpse, as if to gently wake him, and loosened the rock around his feet. The body floated downriver, far in the opposite direction to where the official version of events placed him, the water finally depositing him on a sandy bank before retreating so that the world might reunite itself with the Count. News of a white-haired, decomposing corpse appearing out of the blue left the royalist authorities in a state of panic and prompted the Carlist commander Ros d'Eroles to instruct the material author of the crime, Pere Baltà, to immediately sever the sexagenarian's head from his bloated body but the fellow, already feeling things had gone too far, was paralysed by fear. Two days later, he was buried in an unmarked grave in the Coll de Nargó cemetery. Later, a doctor in phrenology located and desecrated the grave in order to get his hands on the skull, a specimen considered to be of great scientific interest and importance. He jotted algorithms, formulas, and symbols all over it until it was completely covered in mathematical signs. In every lump he saw confirmation of Espagnac's eccentricity, the definitive physical explanation for his absurd life, and the reason behind the glacial calm of that criminal-idealist-officer-terrorist-lunatic lowlife. If we are to believe the story, the skull then found its way into the possession of another phrenologist, Marià Cubí, and then travelled onto the Philippines before being reunited with the rest of its body and laid to rest in the family tomb on the island of Mallorca. But I have gone too far and none of this forms part of the story I wish to tell, therefore I shall retract the above but reiterate the following: this man, who lived and died in such strange circumstances and who swung so erratically between avidity and apathy, was responsible for defending Solsona from the parliamentarians.

A histrionic speech introduced the third twist of fate.

'News, foreign sir, news! I stand before you as spokesman of the military high command. I did profess to you that as a polyglot you could entrust me to entrust myself with your noble and notable request. My words have gone skipping like spring lambs from here to the high command, from the high command to His Most Excellent Royal Highness, from His Most Excellent Royal Highness to Providence, from Providence to His Most Excellent Royal Highness, from His Most, so on and so forth. And now they've returned home! *Elles sont revenues, monsieur!* My, it's been one helluva journey, not without its fair share of detours and setbacks, which explains why it took so long, but it's arrived just when we needed it most. So, without further ado,' he said with a twinkle in his eye, 'it gives me great pleasure to announce that you've been assigned a platoon to defend King, Catholicism, so on and so forth! A platoon, dear sir, so you can finally exercise your military calling, so you can give free rein to your sense of duty!' He paused a moment and hesitated, as though wishing to take back the phrase and polish it a bit but he pressed on regardless. 'The horsemen of destruction are drawing ever nearer, sir, but we shall be saved thanks to you, your troops and my role as mediator.' With his eyes as big as dinner plates, a patently false smile and an infantile intonation, he asked, like someone washing their hands of some ghastly task: 'Are you pleased?'

Wielemann was standing in the doorway to the widow's house with Soler observing him from a distance, either because the house frightened him or to separate himself from his words and oblige them to fend for themselves. He was tense, cowering slightly and had his fists clenched, ready to flee if necessary, while he went on repeating that magical word – 'platoon' – which did nothing but reverberate in Wielemann's ears like artillery fire. Like an adult with a small child, Soler indicated for him to follow with a flick of his hand and took a few steps backwards. Wielemann felt a pain in his mouth. Soler continued to retreat, not once taking his eyes off the Prussian, and inflated his words with enthusiasm: '*Venez, monsieur, venez. Je vous montrerai le peloton.*' They went down the street together and after a series of zigzags came to the Plaça Sant Joan where six men were slouched around the fountain.

'Boys, here's your new commanding officer. *Señor*, I humbly present you with your platoon. Consummate soldiers, the lot of them. Not a single amputated limb between them.' Soler then gave a few approving and hearty slaps on a soldier's leg.

There was the massive fellow with the pale face and swollen cheeks, lurching from side to side as though he were too heavy for his own legs, the tall, olive-skinned man who rolled his Rs heavily and the other four, all equally as short but of contrasting widths: the blonde and chubby one, the not quite as chubby one with the few remaining ginger hairs, the one of average width and discreet in a way that was out of tune with the others, and the gawky one with thick spectacles. Wielemann and the Shambolic Six stared at each other in bemusement.

'Bloody hell, Puss in Boots is back.'

'Just look at the state of dem now.'

'What, and he's s'posed to be in charge of things? If he ain't worked a single day in his bleeding life. I've seen princesses' arses rougher than his hands.'

'He's killed about as many Lib'rals as you've seen princesses' arses, that's for sure.'

Whingebag went and stood inches from Wielemann, propped himself up on his tiptoes and inspected him carefully from behind his steamed up spectacles. A long silence descended over them all. Too long, in fact.

'They have experience, *señor*,' intervened Soler. 'Come on, boys, tell our foreign friend one of your heroic war stories. Lard Arse? Carrot Top?'

'Go on, tell him about… you know…' said the chubby one to his ginger comrade.

'Ah, well, it were nuffin'. We won down at Riner, that's all.'

'Tell him the whole story, man.'

'Well, we were behind some rocks. We had the Lib'rals straight up ahead. They was shooting at us the whole time. We'd been there hours. And then…'

The other five were hanging on his every word.

'… and then I heard the call of nature.'

All five of them burst into howls of laughter.

'Where do you get these fancy words from?'

'From the priest.'

'Come on, soldier, you can tell it better than that,' said Soler while peering at Wielemann out of the corner of his eye.

'Ah, it were nuffin' like. There we was, crouched behind the rocks, all hunched up, for ages, and I could feel me guts cramping up. I wanted to stretch me legs a bit, so I get up and I go over to the bramble, keeping me eye out for the thorns and bullets. Then someone shouts at me from the other side: "What the bleeding hell you doing, Valeri?" Turns out it's me cousin. "I heard the call of nature, Pere," I tell him. Then he half gets to his feet and shouts: "Get yourself over this side, lad. You won't last two minutes out in the open like that." "I can't," I say. "I'm with the Carlists." "Listen, these lot pay a pretty penny, you know what I mean?" he says. "Is that so?" I say. "I heard the Lib'rals don't pay sod all." "Come off it! These lot are rolling in it. We're getting five reals a day over here." We had to shout a lot, out there in the open, on account of the bullets, you see. "How much they paying yous lot?" he asks and I say to him: "I ain't got the foggiest. The lads signed up and I went with them. You know

I'm useless with money. One of the boys takes care of all that. That chubby one over there behind the rock."'

'And us lot,' interrupted Lard Arse with a huge smile, 'we was giving it to dem the whole time.'

'That's when me cousin says: "Come with us, lad. You'll end up with more holes than a sieve out here in the open." I tried to turn and go back but I'd really got meself in a spot of bother. The bullets were whizzing past me and I kept losing me balance on account of it. "Come on, lad! Get yourself over here with us. I already said they pay good." But then I turn and I see the boys, like a dog with two tails the lot of them, shooting with that special feeling you get when the sun's shining and you've had a good breakfast. So I says to me cousin: "I can't, Pere. Me legs wouldn't allow it. Those Lib'rals turn me stomach. Don't get me wrong, there're lads on our side that make me sick but with the Libr'als it's different, it's like there's a ball of fire in me guts, you know?" "It ain't that bad, surely? There're plenty of plain-speaking lads over here and they ain't no different to you and me." Then I feel me face going all red and hot. "Crikey, Pere, you remember Grandpa Toni, don't you?" "Course I do." "You remember when we used to help him with the harvest and then carry the wheat up to the monast'ry and there was that monk who used to give us a proper hiding but there was that other one who always had the hiccups and used to give us chocolate and we used to hide in the cloister and along the corridors and sneak into the refect'ry and drink wine out of the friars' *porró* and afterwards get lost and end up goodness knows how in the chapel and then we suddenly had all the saints and the Virgin Mary looking at us and we'd leg it scared out of our wits and outside we'd catch sight of Solell's daughter with the blond hair who'd just left the tithe and we'd chase her like mad dogs but she always got away and after downing half a *porró* in one go Grandpa Toni would go lie down in the field behind the monast'ry and fall asleep under God's sun and he always worked hard and slept good and the priest always said he had a face full of grace like a happy saint and when he snored it were like the cathedral bells? Do you remember all that, Pere? Did you like all of that?" "Course I did." "Well, the Lib'rals went and burnt it all. No more monks, nor more dark corners to hide in, no more little blonds who catch your eye and run away. Not even Grandpa Toni's snores. I don't understand how you can go with those sons of bitches." The last bit I had to scream like a mule 'cos the bullets were ringing in me ears and they must've been shooting directly at me or sumfin'. "So, Pere," I says, "you coming with us or what?" and the whole time he's looking around him, not knowing what to do and I'm waving at him and finally he starts edging over to me and everything's going trific until Whingebag goes off his rocker.

'It's true. He starts running through no man's land like a headless chicken shouting about the crashing wheel of time and how he's going deaf.'

'And, obviously, the Lib'rals ain't got a clue what's going on. And there's me, out in the open, calm as you like, I'm dodging the bullets, me cousin next to me and Whingebag flapping his arms and shrieking like he's possessed or sumfin'. Must happen all the time to the Lib'rals, mind. They think they know it all but they don't know nuffin'. They were so confused they forgot to shoot and everything. And that's when the boys jump out from behind the rocks and send a whole load of them to kingdom come. The ones who didn't catch a bullet legged it sharpish and I hug me cousin 'cos we'd won but then I hear a strange noise and Pere falls to me feet and his eyes go all cloudy.'

The rest of the Shambolic Six stared at the floor while Josep Soler adopted a solemn expression and went over to shake the man's hand.

'I congratulate you on your cousin's courage and heroism. We shall all get our just rewards in the City of God for our sufferings in this life. I commend you for heeding the call of duty.'

'Oh, no, it weren't the call of duty, sir, it were the call of nature.'

Soler turned away, pretending not to have heard.

'You are now privy, sir, to your platoon's selflessness, proof that you will be able to count on these fine young men come what may. I shall now take my leave so you may familiarise yourselves one with the other.'

His exaggerated bow was accompanied by a long sigh of relief and he quickly disappeared in the direction of city hall.

Wielemann and the Shambolic Six averted their gazes, not wanting to look at one another, while an insurmountable wall of silence rose up between them.

22

Wielemann was woken by the swallow's hysterical chattering. Having slept no more than three hours, his body felt like planks of wood haphazardly pieced together. He turned over on the blanket (the only thing separating him from the cold cathedral floor), coughed and noted the swelling in his mouth again. It was a malignant, merciless pain that immediately extinguished all other thoughts and concerns.

He got up in search of anisette and spotted, slumped by the opposite wall, five of the Shambolic Six busy snoring. A lumpy, undulating mass spread the length of the nave made up of the exhausted exhalations of two-hundred slumbering soldiers heroically resisting waking up. Spread out on the carpet next to the altar in the mellow morning light was Manuel Tell de Mondedéu, Military Governor of Solsona and the man charged with defending the city from the imminent Liberal assault. He was sleeping like a baby.

Nothing surprised Wielemann anymore. It was four days since pro-Christina forces had surrounded the city and one day since they had managed to breach a part of its defences and begin occupying the houses to the west. The Carlists positioned on the hills waiting for them had not so much as lifted a finger and it's hard to say if this strange form of discipline imposed on them by the new high command of the Principality of Catalonia terrified them, made them weary or simply left them indifferent. The last anyone knew of the Count of Spain he was enjoying a slap-up meal at a local tavern. There were barely five-hundred soldiers, including amputees, left in the whole of Solsona and they had all taken refuge either in the palace of the deceased bishop or in the cathedral. They kept watch, slept, and fretted over how far the pro-Christina army had advanced. Occasionally, two Carlist soldiers went out on patrol and only one came back.

Mondedéu remained tight-lipped.

Wielemann watched him in his saintlike sleep. When he saw him for the first time, speaking with Josep Soler outside the doors to the city hall, he didn't seem of this world. He had his head leaning slightly backwards, his eyes half closed and was looking at his interlocutor as though he were miles away in the distance. Rather than moving, he swayed slowly from side to side like a thin branch in the breeze while Soler bombarded him with his verbal artillery and turned from time to time to point towards the silent Prussian. When Soler ceased his attack, the governor raised his chin in the direction of Wielemann as if to sum up, accept and authorise the inevitable, and marched off down the street. And that was that. Wielemann had not seen him anymore forthcoming in front of his troops and he limited himself to strolling past the men and saluting them austerely. When he slept he was equally as equanimous, even with the enemy breathing down his neck.

Wielemann sat down on the floor. A few men had since got up and were grumbling and swearing in the middle of the cathedral. Mondedéu's forefinger began to twitch with tiny spasms but he went on sleeping like a stone. Too many times had Wielemann attempted to decipher the method behind all the madness around him to do anything more than acquiesce and the time had arrived to let fate run its course. Besides, the city was all but deserted now. The widow and the man-child had left more than a week ago and Foraster's grandmother wasn't far behind. The doctor also mentioned leaving sooner rather than later but that if he were to stay, he would shut himself away in his house and refuse to come out until humanity quit blowing things out of proportion. There was an exodus towards the homes of relatives in the surrounding villages and the sheer number of abandoned houses, along with the buildings burnt during the Carlist conquest, meant the city was little more than a series of stone spectres. The most eye-catching sign of human presence were the black flags draped along the walls and the sheet flying above the bell tower bearing the motto VICTORY OR DEATH.

Suddenly, as if some device had activated him, Mondedéu opened his eyes and sat up to reveal a towering stature, almost pompous in its height, which clashed with Wielemann's memory. After offering him a bottle of anisette as though he had been waiting there patiently for that express purpose, he gave what was Wielemann's very first order: he and his troops were to patrol the area around Pont Gate. The news pleased Wielemann but it also left him stunned, not merely for the simple fact that, after a year of waiting, he had finally received an order, and one that was both clear and sensible too, but because the governor had addressed him in flawless German and, on top of that, with a Prussian accent. There was, of course, the chance he had imagined it, but it was well over a year since he had last heard his mother tongue and the phonemes had sounded too real to be a delusion. He turned around in the direction of Mondedéu but the man had already disappeared. Feeling the pain in his mouth reaching gigantic proportions, he took a long, deep swig from the bottle.

The mounds of sprawling bodies began moving under the blankets with the same concealed intensity as a sack full of writhing cats and Wielemann was forced to slalom between them to reach the entangled Shambolics sound asleep on the other side of the nave. The pain in his mouth was like a long, sharp needle jabbing deeper and deeper and he realised that if he was going to shout he would have to bore down far into his core to extract the energy necessary to overcome the acute discomfort. He went outside for some much needed air. There were four drowsy soldiers standing guard in the square as the swallows whizzed past them like arrows. The calm of the city under siege had a magical quality to it. The central fountain gurgled softly and Wielemann downed another shot of anisette. As he began to head back inside, his father's voice called his name.

He spun around in a cold sweat but immediately turned and headed towards the cathedral, only for his father to shout out to him again in his unmistakable voice, so rasping and severe it cut through you like a handsaw: 'Don't forget!' Wielemann rushed over to the street corner to survey the area only to be left feeling inexcusably stupid. All the while the needle plunged relentlessly deeper.

Once back inside the cathedral, he positioned himself directly in front of the Shambolics and, ploughing through the pain, woke them up at the top of his voice. Their entangled limbs twitched and then stretched as they peered slowly and serenely out from their blankets, wondering what all the commotion was about, only to immediately close their eyes again. Spurred on by rage, Wielemann yelled once more, this time jabbing them with the sorry excuse for a rifle he had been issued with the week before. He asked where Whingebag was.

'I wouldn't count on him if I was you,' someone muttered, and a wave of shrugging shoulders moved through the group.

As they sat leaning against the wall, they had the appearance of five demented beggars.

'What I'd like to know is who ordered us here in the first place.'

'He's standing right in front of you.'

'Yeah, well, we'll see how long that lasts.'

None of them showed the least intention of getting up. Under normal circumstances, Wielemann would have given up but the pain maintained him in a state of implacable fury and he violently dragged them outside. They huffed and puffed but, once outside, it was as though the balmy July morning had replenished their vitality, leaving them like beer kegs on the verge of spouting their frothy content and, in an instant, they had switched roles: Wielemann shuffled along, the pain and fatigue almost bringing him to his knees, whereas the Shambolics strode assuredly with their faces pointed towards the sun, stretching their arms and wiggling their fingers. Wielemann edged along the dim, narrow street, followed by the merry disorder of his troops. With a deep sense of foreboding, he stopped next to the side entrance to the cathedral and looked up at Saint Augustine lying in a perpetual state of ecstasy. A voice coming from another street had got trapped within the confines of the square, made louder yet more distant by the echoes: it was his father's voice again, this time with cries of order and discipline, commanding him to serve the State, to esteem the family's military legacy and to love legitimate and redemptive Europe, substantiated over the centuries. Wielemann spun around to see where those chilling words were coming from. More than ever they were empty shells transmitting nothing but he had no other option now but to obey them, to obey them with superhuman strength in contempt of the pain and the ridiculous individuals besieging him. He signalled for them to advance and they followed behind him. The houses eyeing them from both sides of the street had been reduced to skeletal, solitary structures wrapped in a silence free from suffering. Wielemann endeavoured to scrutinise each and every corner but the brief moments he was distracted from the pain in his mouth he had to endure the agony of knowing that anything he failed to spot could cost them their lives. When they reached the Dominican seminary the Shambolics slumped to the ground. Wielemann remained upright owing to the pain but when he heard shouts and whistles coming from nearby he immediately wedged the rifle hard against his shoulder and took aim. The Shambolics remained unperturbed as they lay back in the warm sun. At that moment, Whingebag came plodding around the corner looking sleepy. Wielemann stared at him steely-eyed.

'I kipped at home. The cathedral floor don't do me any favours.'

Wielemann had just enough time to consider it not worth shooting despite his deepening sense of futility. He took another long drink from the bottle.

'You've got some cheek, lad.'

'Leave off! You can't expect me to fight when I've got backache.'

'Oi, how about a bit of respect for the Russian, eh? Look at the bloody state of him. If he didn't look like a ghost before, he certainly does now. And he spent the whole night on the cathedral floor like a man.'

'Nah, you don't get it. It's better I didn't sleep there 'cos now I'm feeling fresh and I can bump off more Lib'rals.'

'Whatever you say, fella.'

'It's true! I'm feeling fit as a fiddle. I'll bump three off, p'raps even four. Mark my words.'

'You and whose army?'

'You'll see! I'll bump five of them off just so they have to give me a milit'ry dickoration.'

The others fell about laughing while Wielemann watched with sweat pouring down his forehead.

'You'll do well to get a dickerection, lad!'

'Even if they did give you a medal you wouldn't know what to do with it.'

'I'd sell it. I know a man who's in that line of business. He'd give me fifty reals for it. Bam! Just like that.'

'How d'you find this fella?'

'You know… out and about.'

'You're fibbing.'

'On the old lady's life! Fifty big ones, I tell you,' said Whingebag, before curling up like an insect playing dead.

Wielemann went over to lean against the seminary wall, hauling his large, inflamed abscess with him.

'And when you get your fifty reals, what you gonna do with dem?' asked Lard Arse enviously.

'Prob'ly buy meself a couple of donkeys and a cart. Dunno. Or a pump for inflating wineskins. I still ain't given it much thought.'

'You don't know if you're coming or going. Look, I'll do you a deal. When you get the fifty, you give me thirty and I'll see you put the rest to good use.'

Whingebag was unsure.

'Listen, I can get you four donkeys and a cart that only needs a bit of fixing up and a fresh lick of paint.'

'Deal,' he said, adopting the serious pose of a businessman.

Wielemann had been gradually stooping lower and lower, desperately clutching his rifle, far away from the group yet keeping a keen eye on things. He could still hear his father's voice, perhaps even clearer than before, and he slowly began to accept the inevitable. It might end well, it might end badly, but it would end. And that was all he wanted. He said yes to discipline and to serving the State, yes to legitimism, yes to his cousin's woeful music. Yes, yes, yes. Just as long as it would all be over.

The Shambolic Six spread throughout the square before disappearing up various adjacent streets but Wielemann no longer cared. The fierce sun permeated everything and a thick, congealing silence suffocated both his soldiers' shouts and his father's whispers. It was over a year since he had arrived in Solsona and the people who had been closest to him – the doctor, Nana, the widow, the man-child – were all now gone. He might very well die there while they waited patiently for everything to go back to normal. He would not be dying for them or against them; he would merely die and that's all. And when it was time to return, they would go back to their homes and continue living like before while retaining the faint memory of a tall, shy Prussian who used to stare at them with his stomach full of so many things to say but which he never dared to utter. And almost certainly his father would stroll along the avenues of Berlin bragging about his son's heroic, meaningful death, a sacrifice on the altar of Order, and the girls would nod and start to daydream while the mothers trembled in silence. But, in reality, it was all the same: a world without him was just as worthy as a world with him. At the end of the day, the good times were dead and buried and even if he did survive, they had already been lost forever. But the abscess – vast, ponderous, and pointed like a castle – erased any memory of them, leaving only his body's physical resistance, the tension of his muscles and nerves and the emptiness in his stomach. The rising sun was even more glorious and inhuman.

'Snake, snake! A viper!'

Lard Arse came bounding down the street, puffing and panting with obese euphoria, causing the others to leap to their feet.

'Where? Where?'

Wielemann looked on in shock at the giddiness that had taken hold of his men. He tensed his body and screamed at them to maintain order but the Shambolics didn't hear and instead went galloping wildly after Lard Arse. Wielemann continued to scream commands until he lost sight of the last man and was left completely alone. He was incandescent with rage.

At any moment the Liberals could mount an attack, but no one had informed him of how far they had advanced. For all he knew, they could be assembling on the other side of the bulwark or about to march around the corner. And there he was, alone, hunched up against the wall, in a mood so despicable that it displaced his desolation. He could hear unacceptable, reckless, outrageous laughter going on and on that he decided he had to put an end to. He sprinted down the street only to find the Shambolics moving in a circle around the snake. Lanky was pelting it with stones and the enraged animal was rearing up and hissing. One of them knocked it back with a branch but it lifted itself up again, raring to poison them all, and they roared with laughter until their bellies hurt. Whingebag abruptly stopped laughing and started shouting and running in circles around the group, out of his mind with fear over the wheel of time, and the others laughed even harder and some of them even began rolling on the floor. When the snake charged towards them they frantically kicked it away, becoming mere fleshy appendixes of their own almighty laughter. Wielemann also felt a mad urge to join in but almost immediately remembered that he was in a bad mood and deep inside him joy and anger faced off in a tense, silent fight to the death that forced him to raise his arms as if wanting to warn someone before hunching over and covering his mouth with both hands as though stricken by some imminent danger. The piercing needle joined forces with his sullen mood and together they vanquished his urge to laugh, humiliating it and chopping it into a thousand pieces of bitter resentment, which they left smeared over Wielemann's face.

Shots rang out and Wielemann's mind turned back to the Liberals. Mining the last dregs of energy from his pain and indignation, he prepared himself for fate to finally play itself out. He shouted like never before, deadening the laughter, perhaps even the snake's rabid anger too, and gave the order to hunt, attack and kill Liberals. To his surprise, the Shambolic Six got into formation and began to quick march like an actual combat unit and Wielemann, in the midst of his suffering, felt a smidgeon of pride and his outlook brightened as he watched the soldiers obey like healthy and responsive extensions of his own body.

The Shambolic Six moved quickly down the street. As Wielemann turned to follow them, he saw something moving out of the corner of his eye and heard a bizarre braying sound. He stopped and saw the man-child come bounding down the street with huge, uneven strides, his eyes a deep red, his huge hands motionless by his side, weeping and howling. It was such a strange, totally unexpected sight that it demanded Wielemann's unmitigated attention. He remained spellbound as the man-child disappeared around the corner leaving him to wonder if it had not in fact been a hallucination. He ran over to the street corner, but he was nowhere to be seen. More gunfire rang out behind him and he ran over to join the Shambolic Six.

From a distance, it was difficult to know exactly what was going on. They were jumping, shooting at a house, running away and creeping back. There was a mechanical sound and then loud thuds and crashes. Something lay completely inert at the

Shambolics' feet like a pile of clothes. Drawing closer, he saw it was a person. There was another crashing noise composed of high and low notes and he realised he was stood in front of the doctor's house.

Wielemann slowed his pace as a couple of Shambolics went inside and he heard a different sound coming from the house now, similar to a tolling bell.

He approached the scene gripped by fear.

The man was curled up on the ground as if to protect himself and Wielemann reached out and touched him but he didn't respond. It was Foraster with two shots to the stomach. He was already dead.

There was another crashing sound and he turned to see the piano come tearing down the stairs and out the door. It tipped over, making an infernal noise as it smashed against the stone slabs. The Shambolics' manic laughter continued as they hurled the enormous pot out of the window, still full of soup. When it hit the street below, it clanged as if the city were splitting in two.

'There's your first dead Lib'ral, mister!'

Wielemann growled with every raging nerve in his body and pointed his rifle at the piano. With his eyes full of stagnant pools of water, he squeezed the trigger for the first time in the war. There was a loud explosion which was then swallowed up by the silence.

23

Long patches of sun slithered like snakes through the grass under an overcast sky. He was certain it was a high plateau because beyond each of the edges was a vertical drop as if the earth, reduced to the dimensions of that meadow, had gone back to being flat and the monsters guarding it had hidden themselves away again below the horizon within the depths of the abyss. A man with a perfectly round face was sat on the grass with a gaze that appeared to be simultaneously focussed on the intricate detail of some nearby object and spying shapes far off in the distance. When the spoon drew near, he would open his mouth, snap it shut with the utensil still inside and not let go until he had swallowed all the soup. The same process then began all over again. The person by his side, feeding him with a benevolent smile, was Wielemann.

'Has he always been this way?' he asked the widow.

She was sitting on the grass, forming a circle with them. The first three humans. Or the last, perhaps. Alone but complete. Soup dripped from the corner of the man's lips and Wielemann reached forwards to dry it with his hand.

'I never dreamt it would be like this.'

The clouds sped quickly across the sky and the earth began to shake.

'You're doing alright for a foreigner. But our son is no Carlist.'

The widow clung to Wielemann and stroked him tenderly. Despite the heat, she was wrapped in a woollen blanket that inhaled and exhaled like a sheep.

'Keep an eye out for a red-headed beggar. We'll have to pelt him with stones if he comes this way. He's trouble.'

The widow smiled gently at him while shaking her head. The earth had begun to slope downwards, forcing the man-child to lean back on one arm. Wielemann managed to avoid spilling any of the soup but, just as he was thinking how well he had managed to adapt to the new situation, the widow spoke to him softly:

'I don't know if you'll ever get used to this. We'll have to tie ourselves together with ropes.'

The earth sloped even more and all three of them began to speed downwards, slipping over patches of sun slipping with them. There was no more pain or suffering. Wielemann kept on trying to feed the man and he wasn't doing so badly given the circumstances. They slipped faster and faster, drawing ever closer to the world's end, just as it was prophesied in the beginning.

Rudolf von Wielemann woke up in a damp, unfamiliar bed in a small room with filthy white walls in an Andorran valley. His head was pounding but the injuries to his arms were superficial. A month later, he was back in Germany. When he walked through the front door, his parents ran to greet him: his mother with relief, his father with satisfaction.

A letter from his uncle was waiting for him. He had already received news of the heroic injuries Wielemann had sustained in the holy defence of throne and altar. The man was proud of him: soon he would have the opportunity to continue the military career he had begun with such aplomb and finesse. The Prussian army needed brave men like him.

24

This morning, I paid a visit to the Solsona city archives, wishing to lose myself among its yellowed and dusty papers and forget the frenzy with which I wrote these last few pages. As I flicked through the death registry for the year 1838, the endless parade of names of the unknown dead comforted me. There were so many that it made death appear insignificant. Our own parade shuffles along as we speak but it's the insignificance of other people's deaths that enables us to go on living.

I did, however, come across one name that wasn't completely meaningless to me. Three days after control of Solsona changed hands, a body appeared on the path to Crow Fountain, laid out upon the white flowers along the water's edge. It was, in the words of the registry, "the simpleton from the widow's house", a child of twenty-seven. Reason of death: unknown. He was buried with a tiny wooden cross in the cemetery next to the Pont Gate, beside one of the cathedral's apsidal chapels. A few years later, in the name of progress, a newer, more spacious, more salubrious cemetery was built on an elevated tract of land on the outskirts of the city and which looked back towards the houses of the living. The tombs of respectable folk were moved there. When they razed the pestilent old cemetery, clinging to the city like a baby to its mother's breast, the man-child's grave was lost forever.

Now, in its place, an old lady crumbles bread for the birds to bicker over on sunny days and at night someone stumbling home after one too many finds it a convenient place to vomit.

A few months after I moved to Lleida, a friend presented me with a 'dictionary' containing words and phrases from *lleidatà*, the local dialect. While the book was very much tongue-in-cheek, it helped change my view of Catalan as a homogenous language and instead regard it as rich, vivid, and morphing with the terrain.

When the central dialect of Barcelona reaches the north-western dialect of Lleida, birds go from being *ocells* to *mixons*, one's grandparents are no longer *els avis* but *los padrins,* and the accents are different enough to become the source of much (good-natured) ridicule between the two sets of speakers. Located in the centre of Catalonia, in the province of Lleida, Solsona is at the transition point between these two dialects and where the dialect of *solsoní* emerges. When I read Garrigasait's novel for the first time, one of the elements that most impressed me was the fact it does something quite uncommon in Catalan literature: the action takes place away from the cultural and linguistic dominance of Barcelona, thus giving a somewhat ignored region a literary platform. Comic exaggeration notwithstanding, I was fascinated to read characters who shared similar linguistic traits with friends and family.

The challenge then was how best to represent this dialect in English without the novel losing its connection to a very specific location. Many of my choices are evidently informed by non-standard usage of the English language, but given this can only take us so far, I found myself asking what exactly is at the heart of *lleidatà* and *solsoní*? My answer was hardiness, humour, and anarchic irreverence. It is this essence that I hope my translation has been successful in communicating.

Aquesta traducció està dedicada a la Flor, sense la qual res no seria possible.